ENTERPRISE™
THE EXPANSE

ENTERPRISE™
THE EXPANSE

Novelization by J. M. Dillard
Based on the episodes "The Expanse" and
"The Xindi" by Rick Berman & Brannon Braga

Based on *Star Trek*® created by Gene Roddenberry
and *Enterprise* created by Rick Berman
& Brannon Braga

POCKET BOOKS
New York   London   Toronto   Sydney   Singapore

POCKET BOOKS, a division of Simon & Schuster, Inc.
1230 Avenue of the Americas, New York, NY 10020

 STAR TREK is a Registered Trademark of
Paramount Pictures.

This book is published by Pocket Books,
a division of Simon & Schuster, Inc.,
under exclusive license from Paramount Pictures.

ISBN: 978-0-7434-8485-5

First Pocket Books hardcover edition October 2003

10 9 8 7 6 5 4 3 2 1

POCKET and colophon are registered trademarks of
Simon & Schuster, Inc.

Manufactured in the United States of America

For information regarding special discounts for bulk purchases,
please contact Simon & Schuster Special Sales at 1-800-456-6798
or business@simonandschuster.com.

This book is dedicated to Margaret Clark,
editor extraordinaire and all-round good soul.

Prologue

On the day the world she knew was destroyed, Liz Tucker was content.

It started as a good day, a happy day. She'd returned home a week earlier from what she and other locals referred to as The Big City—which meant any metropolitan area outside the Florida Keys. Miami, Chicago, Los Angeles—all of them were alike, all crammed with people and homogenized high-tech corporate office buildings, the unimaginative streets filled with ground-car traffic, the skies with skimmers.

It was Liz's job—as she saw it, anyway—to make those cities a little less homogenized, to give the buildings some character, some uniqueness, a design and style that broke with the ubiquitous sleek high-rises that made every city look the same. *Boxes*, Liz called them. No matter how slender and sleek they became, no matter how far they rose into the clouds or how brightly they gleamed—with their solar silver surfaces, reflecting heat in summer, collecting it in winter—they were still boxes, and people should not have to live or work or eat or love in boxes.

Businesses and personal clients soon learned to call on Elizabeth Tucker, AIA, only if they wanted something new, something different. Not a high-rise surrounded by a green grass lawn and moving sidewalks.

Which was one reason Liz was happy at the moment: she'd received news less than an hour before that her design, one of several bids, had just been accepted by Wel-Tech, one of the hemisphere's largest health firms. It was a major assignment: a trinity of offfice buildings connected by a landscaped park. Liz had convinced them to go with strictly indigenous plants and to add a small lake, which would attract native waterfowl. She would be able, finally, to help Chicago look more like *Chicago*, instead of every other city in the world. There would be ducks, swans, geese.

She was happy, too, simply to be home. Before work commenced on the project, she had a few days to herself to relax.

Which meant that she was currently thirty feet below the Gulf of Mexico's surface with her scuba gear. Just the basics: no need for a wetsuit here. The turquoise water was tepid against her skin. *Warm as bathwater,* amazed tourists always said.

There was no place in the world like the Keys; she was proud to be a local, a Conch. Fifty years ago, it had become a total tourist trap: fast food joints, strip shopping malls, wall-to-wall cheesy hotels lining the fragile, narrow coastline, hiding any view of the gulf. The place had been filled with people who wanted nothing more than to play golf, rub coconut-scented oil on their bodies, sit in the sun, and get unrelentingly drunk, people who had no appreciation for the special environment, for the unique wildlife, both of which had been endangered by pollution and other acts of human idiocy.

All that had changed now. Liz's house—a historic landmark, a 1950s bungalow a short walk from the glittering shoreline—was one of several in a quiet neighborhood punctuated by native flora and fauna: fat, squat royal palms, fan-shaped palmettos, flame-colored hibiscus and birds-of-paradise, graceful white herons, and the occasional flamingo grazing for bugs on the front lawns.

She'd grown up in that house; her parents had left it to her when it became clear that her brother didn't want it. Trip had always wanted to explore space; Liz had always made fun of him for it. *What, Earth not good enough for you?* He had taught her how to scuba dive, and when she'd been fascinated by the beauty of it, the sense of weightlessness, the freedom and excitement of exploring a totally different world, he'd said, *Understand now? Space is like this . . . free and open, and full of things no one's ever seen before.*

And Liz had retorted, *Big difference. There are coral reefs here, and fish and a million other things to look at, all nice and close together. Space is filled with a whole lot of nothing. A lot of nothing between all those stars. It's cold and empty, and you can't even breathe.* . . .

He'd gotten her on that point. *Can't breathe underwater, either. Does that mean we never should have invented oxygen tanks?*

And then he started talking about his favorite subject, warp drive, which made the spaces between the stars seem a whole lot smaller. He talked about the possibility of life on other planets; if home was this great, what about the millions of other planets that had to be out there? And all the different types of fascinating aliens . . . The Vulcans weren't the entire universe, you know.

Liz wasn't interested. She loved the Keys, loved Earth, and wanted to make the places she loved better; that was that.

Diving always made her think of her big brother; she smiled, lips pressed tightly together to avoid gulping in stinging, bitter seawater, as she swam beside a huge manta ray, its boneless body undulating gracefully. She wondered where Trip was at the moment, whether he was exploring a planet as beautiful as the undersea world he had introduced to her. She'd taken the boat out, and at the moment, was swimming toward a coral reef, one of her favorite spots, always filled with an intriguing cast of characters.

Liz never got there.

The seafloor beneath her shuddered, sending up pulses of cooler water from deep below; a school of silver tarpon surged upward past her, caught in the strange rising current. She was caught too, catapulted to the surface. The tide was so strong, her mask was forced up to her forehead; she lost her mouthpiece. When she came at last to the surface, she grabbed the side of the boat and gasped for air. It stank of smoke, of something scorched. Liz got a good look back at the shore, and gasped again.

The far side of the island was engulfed by a wall of flame—stretching from the horizon up into the sky, blotting out the sun. The fire-wall was kilometers wide. It gouged deep into the earth, spewing debris in its wake—everything, every life form, incinerated beyond recognition.

And it was *moving*, with the inexorability of a tornado, towards Liz and the gulf.

Oddly, she felt no fear. What she saw was too incomprehensible, too massive; what she felt was awe. At the very least, the Key on which she lived—on which her neighbors lived—would be obliterated.

Overhead, the dazzling sky was momentarily darkened by a rush of seabirds fleeing: cranes, pelicans, gulls. Their cries were drowned out by the roar of the destruction.

Krakatoa, Liz thought. *An entire island blown away without warning by a volcano. One day there, the next, gone.* The birds had been first to leave there, too.

But the wall of fire encroached too methodically, at too even a pace, to be a natural phenomenon. This horror was man-made; or perhaps, Liz considered, designed by a hand other than man's.

The gulf began to grow warmer than the smoke-filled

air. Liz's impulse was to replace her mask and breathing gear, and dive down where it was cooler—but a strong current kept her pinned to the surface, trapped near other unwilling victims: a pair of chattering dolphins, the school of now-thrashing tarpons, a struggling barracuda.

Get in the boat, her mind finally told her, cutting through her shock. *Get in the damned boat and get the hell out of here.*

White-foamed waves crashed against her and the small power-boat as the wall of flame neared. The current was so strong by this time that trying to find the ladder, clinging to it with her arms, took agonizing effort. She managed to pull herself up—just enough to try lifting her leg up, stepping into the boat . . .

A great wave came along, and capsized it, forcing Liz for an instant beneath the water's surface. She bobbed up again, coughing, and opened her eyes, stinging from the salt. The boat was designed to right itself instantly—but another wave caught it, and overturned it again, and a third swept it away from her reach. By this time, the sea was so rough, she could do nothing but tread water.

Liz began to sweat, despite the fact that she was submerged up to her chin. She had hoped, up to that point, that the water would protect her—but it was beginning to roil from the heat.

She watched, amazed, as the stream of fire from the sky devoured the shore and any creature hapless enough to remain there.

Then it found the water's edge. A deafening hiss followed as steam rose high beyond the clouds, mixing in with the smoke; as Liz watched, the ocean *disappeared*, foot by foot, replaced by an ugly, fathomless crater.

Her skin grew red, scalded, as she watched the fire come closer. Her first thought, the more maudlin one, was that if she had to die, at least she was dying in the place she loved best.

Her second and last thought was, *Bet Trip has seen nothing as wild as this, even out in space* . . .

Chapter 1

He was a Xindi warrior, of his culture's highest class, and out of a sense of decorum he had worn his ceremonial armor on this, his last mission, though he would not need it, and though it could not protect him from his fate.

He had already attended his own death ceremony, already been honored for the heroic deed he would perform on behalf of his people, his homeworld, against the Enemy-to-come. Then, he had felt only a sense of pride. He had been accorded every pleasure, every desire: his kin were left behind with great prestige and wealth. They would build monuments to his memory.

Now he sat in the Enemy's home system, at the controls of the destroyer/probe. It was a handsome craft: two concentric spheres, each as perfect as his world, each rotating within the other. It had two functions: the first, to send information to his leaders; the second, to destroy.

The warrior passed through the alien solar system

without difficulty, and sped toward his target: the planet -where the Enemy-to-come dwelled, unaware as yet of its future crime. The world itself—*Earth*, an ugly word, bitter on the tongue—was not as hideous as the warrior had imagined, with its swirls of blue and green. There was, in fact, an odd beauty to it. For an instant, the warrior permitted himself to consider the life-forms dwelling there, on the green landforms, in the blue oceans: They were unaware of the crimes that would be perpetrated by their heirs, and therefore not guilty. The Xindi knew nothing of their culture: perhaps they were not so different from his own people.

He censored the thought at once: Such reflection was dangerous, and could only hinder his mission.

He slowed his vessel, and dropped down into the lower atmosphere, confident that he would not be detected, given the primitive science of the natives.

He programmed the targeted area—a peninsula and island in the western hemisphere—into his weapon's sites. All went as he had practiced in the hundreds of simulations, yet he could not shake a feeling of displacement, of anxiety—was it caused by his great distance from his homeworld, or was it cowardice in the face of his own demise?

The ancient ceremonial armor, thicker and heavier than the sleek battle armor to which he was more accustomed, made his fingers feel thick, even clumsy, as he pressed the controls; beneath it, his scales had grown overheated. Since there was nothing he could do to help his body cast off the unwanted heat, he shrugged off all concerns about himself—they were, at this stage, useless—and watched, with grim delight, as the weapon performed exactly as designed.

He glanced at a small monitor showing the destroyer/probe from the exterior: The concentric spheres rotated into position so that the emitters lined up perfectly.

The deck beneath his feet began to hum as the weapon powered up. He watched the bitter-named Earth on the viewscreen as a blast of pure destruction streamed from his vessel and strafed the island and peninsula, as well as the body of water where they rested. Even from the stratosphere, the warrior could see plumes of steam rising from the sea, black smoke streaming up from the land.

Marvelous; just as in the simulations.

The warrior finished his task with a sense of accomplishment, and sent the triumphant information back to his leaders: the weapon had worked precisely as designed. So this had been the source of his anxiety: the possibility of failure. Now that it was gone, he feared nothing.

He received back a prerecorded message of congratulations and farewell.

He programmed his vessel to self-destruct without hesitation or reluctance. He did not think of his children, his mates, his parents, or his fellow warriors. He did not, in fact, permit himself to think at all. He merely braced himself physically for what was to come, and when at last the destroyer/probe imploded, there was no time even to flinch.

He was, like his victims on the surface, killed immediately, his scale-covered flesh seared in a blindingly bright millisecond. However, an explosive in the vessel's engine failed to ignite; the exterior of the destroyer/probe remained intact, and tumbled towards the planet surface—evidence for alien hands to paw over, alien minds to contemplate.

Even his corpse failed to be incinerated—more evidence, to indicate the involvement of his species.

Had the warrior lived to know this, he would have been deeply disappointed.

Chapter 2

With a warrior's fierce stoicism, Duras, son of Toral, stood upon the dais before the Klingon High Council. He did not permit shame that had gnawed at him for months to show; indeed, at times it had come close to overwhelming him, and he had almost yielded to the temptation to end his life at his own hands.

Two things had stopped him: the possibility of revenge so long as he lived, and the shame that suicide without honor would bring to his family. So long as there was any hope of revenge, he would live for that moment.

After many unsuccessful petitions, and months of Duras grinding his teeth, the Council had at last agreed to see him. Duras had returned to his home planet to appear before the Council members; it had been a long journey from the Ty'Gokor defense perimeter, a place for the incompetent, the humiliated, the disgraced.

Those who worked there—and, unfortunately, many

who didn't—referred to it as *the latrine of the Empire*, the place where all refuse was funneled.

Duras had never appreciated the metaphor.

Now he stood and listened with respect and forced patience to the words of the chancellor, who stood in the central position of honor amidst the other members.

"Twice!" the chancellor roared, emphasizing the word by striking the podium with his great fist. Silver hair spilled past his venerable shoulders; he was broad of build, broad of face, still thick of bone and muscle. His very presence emanated the power that was rightly granted him. Even Duras, in his prime and strong, doubted he would emerge the victor in hand-to-hand combat with the ancient warrior.

"Twice he's been captured," the chancellor continued, his mighty baritone ringing off the walls of the great chamber, "and twice he's escaped! Our magistrate should never have shown him mercy! He should've been executed for his crimes!"

Duras did not need to ask to whom the chancellor referred: the name had burned in his mind and heart with peculiar venom, ever since he had been sent to Ty'Gokor. *Archer.*

Archer, the human who had destroyed his honor, his life.

Not so long ago, Duras had been the proud, invincible captain of the *Bortas*, one of the Empire's finest vessels. The chancellor had given him a command: retrieve the rebels who had fled the Klingon protectorate of Raatooras, and bring them to justice.

It had seemed a simple enough task—until Archer and his ship, the *Enterprise*, had interfered. The human had "rescued" the starving rebels, whose ship was in disrepair—then had broken Klingon law and insulted Duras by refusing to turn the rebels over.

Duras responded by firing his weapons. It should have been an easy matter of crippling the Earth ship—Duras's battle cruiser was clearly the superior vessel—then seizing the rebels, and finishing the humans off.

Archer, however, was both treacherous and cowardly. Rather than fight boldly, he sailed his ship into the nearby planetary ring system, then used explosions to create a plasma that blinded Duras's sensors and temporarily crippled his weapons.

Then he fled, taking the rebels with him.

To deepen the outrage, Archer did not even perform the courtesy of destroying Duras and the *Bortas*. Instead, the Klingon captain was forced to return in failure to his chancellor.

Duras hoped for death; such grace was not permitted him. Instead, he was demoted to second weapons officer, and sent to the underbelly of space. His kin was shamed, and no longer spoke his name.

They had managed to capture Archer, and bring him before a tribunal on the outpost Narendra III. Duras had appeared and engaged the empire's best prosecutor, Orak. Confident of victory, confident that his position as captain would be restored, Duras had watched the trial— only to be aghast when an all-too-lenient sentence was handed down. Archer was sentenced to labor in the dilithium mines on the ice world, Rura Penthe—but once again, human treachery intervened.

Archer escaped, and Duras was left to remain a lowly weapons officer.

Now, standing on the dais before the High Council, a muscle in Duras's left jaw spasmed, the only outward sign of the hatred that consumed him. He lived only to redeem his house; he lived only to kill Archer.

A Council member spoke, his tone dripping with condescension. "You had a simple mission, Duras: locate the rebels Archer was harboring and return them to the empire. But you failed. Archer made a fool of you!"

Duras permitted himself no reply; the words that sprang to his firmly compressed lips would have cost him his life.

At last, the chancellor uttered the words Duras had long yearned to hear.

"We are offering you a chance to regain your command, and your honor."

So; the decision had been made in his favor. Duras let go a long breath of pure satisfaction.

"I will not fail!" he swore to the chancellor.

In his mind's eye, he saw the *Enterprise*, charred and floating, dead in space.

Aboard the *Enterprise*, Chief Engineer Charles "Trip" Tucker entered the conference room and immediately knew something was wrong, very wrong.

Even before he received the summons to the conference room, the ship had slowed to impulse—which probably meant communications were coming in from Earth. He'd thought nothing of it, had assumed it meant a new mission, some new chore they'd thought up at HQ. He'd been in engineering running maintenance on the warp drive, and for some odd reason thinking of Lizzie.

Remembering times from long ago: thirteen-year-old Lizzie. Trip had been almost seventeen then, and he had caught her kissing a kid two years older than she was, a skinny sophomore who he knew from the local high school—what was his name? Carlo something. He was a whiz at botany, that kid; he had actually been in the same class with Trip and the other seniors.

Carlo, all elbows and knees, and Trip had flipped his lid when he found skinny Carlo in a liplock with his little sister behind the movie theater.

Hey, he'd yelled, as he grabbed the kid by the shoulder and pulled the two lovebirds apart. *Why don't you go pick on someone your own age?*

Lizzie'd been furious. *Hey, leave him alone, Trip.*

Get out of here! Trip had shouted, ignoring his sister, and Carlo obeyed, taking flight.

He and Lizzie had fought like the dickens then—he wasn't sure who was madder at whom, but all of his protective big-brother instincts had come to the fore that day.

Tucker grinned at the memory. Funny, how back then two years had made poor frightened Carlo seem like a sophisticated man of the world, out to take advantage of his baby sister. Of course, knowing Lizzie, it was hard to say who was taking advantage of whom. Lizzie had always insisted she was perfectly capable of taking care of herself. Didn't Trip trust her?

Trip trusted her, all right; no one had a sounder head on her shoulders than Lizzie. It was the guys he had the problem with. Being a guy himself, he knew they were up to no good.

Tucker's reverie had been interrupted then, when a call came, asking him to report to the conference room immediately.

Trip entered and found the Vulcan Science Officer T'Pol, Lieutenant Malcolm Reed, Doctor Phlox, Hoshi, and Mayweather, all standing around the table.

Standing, not sitting and talking casually. The expressions—save for T'Pol's, of course, which was always blandly passive—were all grim. Something major was up, and it wasn't good.

"What's going on?" Trip asked.

"The Captain wants to talk to us," Reed said somberly. His British accent seemed even more pronounced than usual—as it often did when he was worried or tense about something, a fact Trip had learned over the course of their friendship.

"About what?"

The linguist and communications officer, Hoshi Sato, was petite and delicate-boned, her long dark hair pulled back at the nape of her neck. Her brow was frankly furrowed with concern. Travis wasn't surprised; she'd always been a bit of a worry-wart, although after logging some experience aboard *Enterprise,* she'd learned to loosen up quite a bit. "He's speaking to Admiral Forrest . . . it's about the third time in the last hour."

"Something's obviously up," Trip said.

Even Doctor Phlox's normally cheery demeanor had vanished. "I can't remember the last time he asked me to join the senior staff for a briefing," the Denobulan said, clearly perplexed. His brow, too, was lined . . . and edged with small skeletal ridges, all the way around the orbital socket. A receding hairline made them all the more noticeable—at least, in Trip's opinion.

"Maybe it has something to do with—" Reed began, but broke off at once as Archer walked into the room. He had a decade and a few inches in height on Trip, but was still lean and fit, younger-looking than his forty-odd years.

Everyone turned toward him.

Trip knew at once that someone had died. More than one person, in fact; many more.

Archer's expression was beyond grim; it was the face of a man trying to digest something which could not be comprehended. It was the face of a man overwhelmed by the news he was about to relay. Trip thought at once of his mother's expression, at the instant she had been forced to tell Trip's dad that his brother had been killed.

"There's been an attack on Earth," Archer said, his voice hoarse, nearly a whisper. He was looking directly at his staff, yet at the same time seemed to be staring at a distant point far beyond them, at a sight too horrific for words. The Captain paused for a long moment, as though he could not find further words to explain what had happened.

Trip heard the surprised gasps around him, but he could focus on no one other than Archer. "What do you mean, attack?" he demanded. At the same instant he asked the question, he felt an odd pricking sensation on the back of his neck, an odd instinct that he was about to hear news that would strike at him personally.

The Captain was clearly struggling not to be stunned himself by the news he relayed. "A probe . . . They don't know where it came from. It fired a weapon that cut a swath . . . four thousand meters long . . . from Florida to Venezuela." He drew in a breath, then added, "There may have been a million casualties."

The word *Florida* pierced Trip like a dagger; he could not keep his jaw from dropping. "A million?" he heard Reed reiterate in disbelief. *Lizzie*, he thought, and the image of her kissing fifteen-year-old Carlo, her blond hair falling forward onto the boy's shoulders, surfaced again in his mind. *No, of course she's okay, don't even think about it. There are millions and millions of people in Florida; chances are she's okay.* Of course *she's okay.*

He had to force himself to follow the rest of the conversation. It was difficult; numbness started to creep over him.

"We've been recalled," Archer continued.

"Did they say why?" The words came out of Trip without his thinking about them; his mind was still repeating the mantra, *She's okay* . . .

Yet he knew, with dreadful, inexplicable certainty, that she was not.

"I didn't ask."

Ensign Travis Mayweather, the helmsman and one of the youngest members of the crew—but the one with the most hours logged in space—spoke up. "It'll take a while to get back, sir."

A voice filtered through the companel. Trip was too dazed even to recognize it. "Bridge to Captain Archer."

Archer tapped the companel. "Go ahead."

"It's Admiral Forrest."

"Understood." Archer turned and headed for the door. As he moved, he glanced over his shoulder back at Mayweather. "Set a course, Travis. Warp five."

He left behind a silent crew.

Inside the ready room, Jonathan Archer stood, arms folded tightly across his chest as if he could somehow hold in the emotions warring within him, and stared out the window at the stars streaming past. Normally, the sight never failed to thrill him—warp speed, achieved at last—but now he saw nothing but Admiral Forrest's lined face, pale against the dark blue-black of his uniform, as he tried to describe the destruction.

The land, the sea, scorched and gouged beyond recognition; ugly craters miles deep. The devastation was so vast, so complete, that it was impossible to know the full extent yet.

And if there can be one attack, Archer knew, *there can be many. Perhaps this is only the first.*

It would be a hell of thing if humanity finally managed to avoid destroying itself, only to be destroyed by another species. It wouldn't be fair. *Just as we were finding our way . . .*

His father, Henry Archer, had devoted his entire career to building a ship that would house Zefram Cochrane's warp drive. *Enterprise* was Henry's baby; he had waited a lifetime to see it launch . . . only to be disappointed. The Vulcans had claimed humans weren't "ready," weren't "mature" enough to interact safely with other species. They had delayed the launch . . . until finally, the son, Jonathan Archer, now her captain, had insisted that *Enterprise* be allowed into space.

By that time, his dad had already died. But the way he saw it, Jon figured he owed it—to his dad, to the human race, to make sure *Enterprise* did what she had been designed to do.

Now everything—the mission, Earth itself—was in jeopardy.

Archer's door chimed. Without turning from the window, he called, "Come in."

He heard the footsteps, heard Trip Tucker's Southern-accented tenor behind him.

"Excuse me, Captain . . ."

"Trip," he said, still without turning.

"When you.spoke to Admiral Forrest . . ."

"Yes?" The stars were still streaming dizzyingly past. Archer wondered if, after their return to Earth, he would ever be able to see them at warp speed again. If there was an even larger attack against Earth, the *Enterprise* might need to be used in combat against alien vessels.

"Did he say what part of Florida was hit?" Tucker pressed.

Archer was still too caught up in his own thoughts to register the personal import of Trip's question. "No, I'm sorry."

"She may have been away." There was a catch in Tucker's voice; he was struggling. "Architects take a lot of trips . . ."

Archer at last heard the undercurrent of pain in his engineer's voice. He pulled himself from his reverie and turned to face Trip.

How could he, Archer, have been so thoughtless? Of course; Tucker's family was from Florida, and from Trip's brotherly tone, Archer guessed they were talking about a sibling. "Older or younger?" he asked—with just enough concern. Too much would make it harder for Trip to maintain his composure.

"She's my baby sister," Trip said. His golden hair was disheveled, as though he had been running his hands anxiously through it.

The words came like a blow. For his friend's sake, Archer did not allow his expression to change; he merely listened as Trip continued.

"When we were in school, I made sure all the boys in her class got a good look at me . . . None of them ever messed with her." He barely managed to finish without choking up.

Archer did not quite smile at the words; he imagined Trip, something of a hell raiser himself, must have made quite a formidable big brother. "Maybe she was away on a trip," he said firmly, insistently, echoing Tucker's hope.

For a time, neither spoke; it was clear Trip didn't believe it.

The engineer lowered his face, got control of himself again, then looked squarely back at Archer. "Anything you can tell me about what the admiral said?" He squared his shoulders, clearly steeling himself for the response.

For the most fleeting instant, Archer considered not revealing everything—but he put himself in Tucker's place. If it were his relative, he would want to know the truth. Reluctantly, he said, "The number of casualties has been revised . . ." He drew a breath. "It's up to three million."

Grief and fury flickered across Tucker's face. "Why would someone do this . . . ?"

There was no answer; Archer did not try to give one. The door chimed again. "Come in," he said.

T'Pol entered. Amazing, Archer thought, that while the Vulcan's face showed no obvious emotion, her movements, voice, and even posture managed to convey compassion toward her stricken crewmates. She seemed to sense at once that Trip was experiencing some difficulty; therefore, her attitude was deferential, as if she realized she was interrupting an emotional moment. Careful to leave Tucker plenty of physical space, she said quietly to the Captain, "I spoke with Ambassador Soval . . ."

"And?" Archer asked.

"A Vulcan transport located the pod in Central Asia. They retrieved it and brought it to Starfleet Headquarters."

Tucker listened with ferocious interest.

Archer at once moved away from the window and stepped up to the Vulcan. "What do they know?"

"Very little," T'Pol replied. "There was a pilot . . . killed on impact."

"Who the hell was he?" Trip demanded, his tone ragged, verging on the desperate. "What species?"

T'Pol's calm demeanor was a stark contrast. "They don't know."

"Did they say anything about what part of Florida?"

T'Pol lifted her eyebrows curiously at the engineer. "No."

Archer explained. "Trip's sister lives in Florida."

T'Pol nodded, understanding. Archer silently blessed her for not bringing up the fact that a Vulcan would not be emotionally overwhelmed by the possible loss of a family member.

The com beeped; Archer was tempted to groan. Whatever it was, it could not be good news. He pressed the companel. "Archer."

Reed's voice filtered through the panel. "Three Suliban vessels just showed up . . . one off starboard, two dorsal."

Even worse news than expected. He'd at least expected to make it home to Earth. Now they were forced to deal with the Suliban, warriors from the future renowned for their deceit, interested only in manipulating the flow of time to their own advantage. They had tried to kill Archer before; whatever they wanted now, it wasn't good.

"Just what we need," Archer muttered, then said, more loudly, to Reed: "Tactical Alert."

As the klaxons blared, the Captain and his two officers headed for the bridge.

Chapter 3

Accompanied by T'Pol and Tucker, Archer stepped onto the dimly lit bridge to see a large Suliban vessel, flanked by two smaller cell ships, on the viewscreen. Hoshi, Reed, and Mayweather were at their stations as the Captain took his chair.

"Hail them," Archer ordered.

Hoshi complied, working her console; after a pause, she turned toward Archer. "They're not responding."

"Try again," Archer said.

In the instant he spoke, he caught movement in his peripheral vision—swift and spiderlike flashes of red. One moved toward him from the side, two overhead.

The Suliban, Archer thought, just before the bridge went utterly dark . . . then vanished completely.

* * *

27

The lights flickered, then came back on.

It was Malcolm Reed who noticed first that Archer's chair was empty; he called out to the others.

"The Captain!"

Archer found himself standing in a small, dimly lit chamber; he had no doubt that he was now aboard the largest of the Suliban vessels, transported there instantaneously courtesy of future technology.

He had hardly time to draw in a breath and orient himself before Silik entered, flanked by two Suliban warriors.

Archer was not surprised; this was not his first encounter with Silik—a high-ranking officer in the Suliban Cabal, a mysterious organization from the twenty-second century, fighting in what he referred to as the Temporal Cold War.

Of all the aliens Archer had encountered, Silik still impressed him as the most exotic-looking. Though his body and features were clearly humanoid, he was entirely hairless, and his skin was a deep shade of olive green, stippled with rust. His eyes were bright, clear orange; combined with his red uniform, it made him an unsettlingly colorful creature.

It was hard to know, however, just how much of that coloration was natural for a Suliban; Silik bragged about his genetic enhancements, which he earned—or lost—depending on his performance as a soldier. He had little love for Archer, who had once cost him his visual enhancements.

Silik spoke immediately after entering, without explanation or greeting. "There's someone who needs to speak with you." He spoke in an elegant, rich bass. *Natural or an enhancement?* Archer wondered. He was lean and fluid in his movements, naturally graceful, and velvety in manner.

Archer looked on him with hatred. It could not be an accident that Silik had chosen to appear now, after the devastation on Earth; clearly, the two were connected. It was easy to envision a scenario where the temporal warrior had decided to conveniently remove certain humans who might one day in the future cause trouble for the Suliban. "I knew you had something to do with this."

Silik's expression was perpetually bland; either he was a master of self-control, or members of his race were not given to showing emotion using their facial muscles. "Do with what?" Impossible to tell whether he was lying— though the Captain had come to learn that most of the time, Silik was.

"Millions of people, Silik!" Archer's tone was vicious, bitter. "You killed millions of people!"

Smoothly, Silik answered, "I'm afraid I don't know what you're talking about."

Outraged, Archer took a threatening step toward the Suliban; the two soldiers stepped forward, weapons raised, and blocked him.

Silik was unmoved by both the specter of violence and the thought of millions of human deaths. In the same self-composed manner, he said, "That wouldn't be wise, Captain."

"What the *hell* am I doing here?" Archer demanded. Grudgingly, he stepped back; the soldiers at once dropped back as well, and lowered their weapons.

"There's someone who needs to speak with you," Silik replied, regarding Archer calmly with his deep-set orange eyes. "He has information you should find helpful. Don't worry, you won't be harmed."

"Information about what?"

"Something to do with your species," Silik said. "It's in great danger." Even while discussing such an emotionally laden subject, he remained unmoved, distant, as though the human race and its fate were rhetorical subjects, centuries away from anything relevant.

Archer did not permit his expression and posture to cease radiating outrage—but Silik's words left him perplexed. The Suliban warrior was not necessarily devoted to the killing of humans, only to whatever gave him and his people the greatest advantage in his Temporal Cold War. This made dealing with Silik extremely difficult, for there were times he actually told the truth.

The question was, was now one of those times?

On the bridge, T'Pol had assumed command.

It was fortunate that Trip Tucker had not; he was prepared to open fire on the Suliban vessel, and said as much. Clearly, his concern for his sister was seriously affecting his judgment.

T'Pol, however, remained calm. The instant it was ascertained that Captain Archer was not aboard the

Enterprise, she had ordered Hoshi to hail the Suliban ship.

The hail was ignored, of course; but T'Pol insisted Hoshi keep trying. In the meantime, she considered possible alternatives. Most likely, Captain Archer was aboard one of the Suliban vessels; attacking them would only endanger him, and was therefore the least desirable course of action.

T'Pol did not have much time to contemplate her next action. Within two minutes, Hoshi's console beeped; she responded, and turned eagerly to face T'Pol.

"It's Captain Archer."

T'Pol gave a single, curt nod.

Hoshi understood the silent command and opened a com channel at once.

"Captain?" T'Pol said, into her companel.

"Hold your position," Archer said. "I don't think we're going to have a problem."

Were T'Pol human, the Captain's words would have surprised her. The Suliban and problems normally went hand-in-hand. However, the Captain's voice betrayed no sign of coercion or duress. T'Pol decided to obey the order.

Trip Tucker, however, could not contain his worry. "Sir?" he asked, half disbelieving.

Archer's tone was reassuring. "It's okay, Trip. Just be patient."

T'Pol was prepared to be as patient as she needed to be; she could not, however, say the same for Commander Tucker.

*   *   *

Silik led Archer to a different chamber, one where he saw a figure he recognized: the dark silhouette of a humanoid—perhaps Suliban, perhaps human or Vulcan, perhaps even Klingon; it was impossible to tell. The silhouette was enveloped by a column of fast-rippling blue light that made Archer dizzy when he stared at it too long.

Archer stopped a distance away.

Silik prodded him. "He can see you more clearly if you move closer."

The Captain refused to budge. "Who is he?"

Rather than reply, Silik said, "He wants to talk to you. It would be foolish to ignore him."

Archer paused. He had played the fool before with Silik, let himself be manipulated, and he did not want to allow that to happen again. Yet the prospect of solving the mystery of what had happened on Earth was too important to ignore. He stepped forward and asked the fig- ure, "What do you want?"

"Your planet was attacked," the humanoid said. His voice was definitely male though higher-pitched, more inflected with emotion, more concerned than Silik's detached bass.

"I'm aware of that," Archer replied.

"What you're not aware of is why." The shimmering figure paused. "The probe was sent by the Xindi. They learned that their world will be destroyed by humans in four hundred years."

"How would they know what's going to happen in four hundred years?" Archer demanded. It was the meddling of characters like Silik and his soldiers—and this mysterious silhouette in his temporal chamber—that caused such problems.

"They were told by people from the future," the figure said evasively. "People who can communicate through time."

"Are they the ones the Suliban are working for?"

"The Suliban work for me," the figure stated flatly.

"So *you're* the one who tried to start a civil war in the Klingon Empire," Archer said, his anger once again rising. "The one who's manipulated my mission from day one . . ."

The humanoid refused to be distracted from the subject at hand. "The people who have contacted the Xindi belong to another faction." He paused to give his next words greater emphasis. "The probe was only a test. The Xindi are building a far more powerful weapon. When it's completed, they'll use it to destroy Earth."

Archer took the thought to its logical conclusion. "Annihilate us . . . before we can annihilate them." The realization was chilling . . . but another question remained. "Why are you telling me this?"

"The Xindi were not supposed to learn about their future . . . If they deploy this weapon, it will contaminate the time-line." It seemed as though the figure faced him and fixed its gaze on him directly. "You mustn't let that happen."

33

Archer felt deep frustration. It was like being caught in a spiderweb; once any time traveler intervened in the past, strands were bound to become tangled, broken. How did the humanoid know that he wasn't contaminating the past even more by informing Archer about the Xindi? "Why should I believe you?"

The answer, for once, was straightforward and simple. "You have no choice but to believe me."

Inside his ready room with T'Pol, Archer was angry and quite unable to keep it from showing.

Silik had, 'for once, kept to his word and returned Archer to his ship; the Suliban vessels had already sped away. Once again, the *Enterprise* was slicing through space at warp five, and the stars were streaming past the window.

And T'Pol was utterly skeptical of Silik's story. She was in full Vulcan mode; eyebrows lifted, expression cold, arms folded across her chest, a physical symbol of her mental rejection. "If this 'time traveler' is trying to protect humanity, why didn't he tell you all this *before* millions of people were killed?"

The question had occurred to Archer as well. Frankly, it troubled him, but he *had* come up with an answer of sorts. "He didn't think we'd believe him." Much to his surprise, his tone was furious, filled with frustration; even more to his surprise, he didn't try to edit the anger out. Millions of people had died, and he was trying to sort the situation out. Damn it, he was trying to *do* something, and he didn't like the fact that in order to try to help the situation, he had to trust Silik and his mysterious leader. So he took it out on T'Pol. It didn't help matters that she was disbelieving. "He's probably right."

The more heated Archer's tone became, the cooler T'Pol grew. "I'm sure Starfleet and the High Command will find a far more logical explanation of who attacked Earth."

That was it; Archer raised his voice. "He may be telling the truth. If he is, I need your support, not your damn skepticism."

She lifted her chin at that.

It was pure instinct, at last, that had convinced Archer, and that was all he had to go on: pure instinct, that the time traveler was telling the truth.

And if he couldn't convince his second-in-command, how was he ever going to convince anyone at Starfleet?

Captain's Starlog, April twenty-fourth, twenty-one fifty-three. The journey home has been very difficult. We've learned that over seven million people have been lost.

"Captain," Mayweather said from the helm, glancing back over his shoulder. The ship had slowed to impulse, now that they were nearing their solar system.

Archer clicked off his recorder and let his gaze follow to where Mayweather pointed. On the viewscreen, one white star shone some three times more brightly than the rest.

"That's our sun," Mayweather explained softly. Child of starfarers though he was—he'd grown up on a space freighter—even the helmsman couldn't keep the sentimentality from his voice. Earth was home, a fact embedded in every human's DNA, even if they hadn't been born on the planet's surface.

The bridge grew silent. Archer took a step forward. It'd been a long time since he last set eyes on old Sol; there was a sense of joy and wonder at seeing it again. When he'd left it behind, filled with excitement at *Enterprise's* launch, he'd wondered whether he'd survive to see it once more.

There was also a sense of sorrow, greeting it under such circumstances. It was far from the happy homecoming he'd imagined.

His reverie was interrupted by the shrill sound of an alarm at Malcolm Reed's station.

"A vessel's dropping out of warp," Reed reported tersely.

"Where?" the Captain demanded.

"Two hundred kilometers off port."

Archer turned to T'Pol, who was already consulting her scanners. "Who are they?"

Reed called out, "They've fired some kind of—"

He never finished. The roar of the blast temporarily deafened Archer; he fought to stay on his feet as the deck shuddered beneath his feet.

He had barely enough time to make it to his chair before the next blast came.

Chapter 4

Through sheer tenacity, Archer managed to hold on as the ship reeled beneath an onslaught of weapons fire. There could be no question: whoever was attacking them was hellbent on destroying the *Enterprise*.

Over the roar of the next blast, and the sound of the ship trying to shake herself apart, Reed shouted, "That one took out both forward phase-cannons!"

"You've still got torpedoes!" Archer called back.

Reed gave a curt nod without looking up from his console and set to work launching a counterattack.

From her station, T'Pol managed to project her voice without shouting or sounding in the least bit alarmed. "It's a Klingon bird–of–prey."

As she spoke, an image appeared on the viewscreen: the Klingon vessel, brilliantly illuminated against the dark backdrop of space by a salvo of Reed's torpedoes. Archer watched in amazement as each burst of light swiftly dissipated, leaving the bird-of-prey unscathed.

We're outgunned, he realized at the precise moment that the Klingon ship released a vicious blast.

The deck heaved, listed violently to the left, then slowly righted itself. The Captain knew instinctively that his vessel had just sustained heavy damage.

Another blow.

Why? Archer asked himself. Certainly, he wasn't popular with the Klingons—but why would they pursue him so far from their own territory? It made no sense to pick a fight here, so close to Earth.

Hoshi turned toward him, her earpiece in place, her gaze unfocused as she listened and translated for Archer. "They want *you,* sir. They're saying that they won't destroy *Enterprise* if you surrender to them."

A loud *boom* silenced her, as the ship shook under another blast. She waited it out, then continued, quoting, " 'Archer is an enemy of the Empire . . .' " She paused, mentally translating. " 'He must be brought to justice if honor is to be regained.' "

Suddenly, Archer understood, at the precise instant the *Enterprise* sustained another hit. Only one Klingon would be desperate enough to pursue him, all the way to Starfleet Headquarters, if need be.

"*Duras,*" he murmured, beneath the flickering bridge lights.

On the Klingon bird-of-prey, Duras was exultant, reveling in the sweet taste of revenge. On the viewscreen before him, he watched as the *Enterprise* listed, her starboard nacelle destroyed, scorched into uselessness by disruptor fire. Soon, Archer would be standing before him, a prisoner, and Duras would have the pleasure of delivering him to the Klingon Council and seeing him properly executed.

It would be a gloriously slow, agonizing death.

From his scanner, Duras's temporary first officer reported, "Both their nacelles are crippled."

"And weapons?" Duras asked. While it seemed obvious the *Enterprise*'s firepower was at least partially compromised, Archer had proven himself quite capable of trickery. Duras wanted to be certain before issuing his next command.

His tactical officer replied. "Their cannons are down."

Duras straightened in his chair, and for a time said nothing, preferring instead to bask in the sense of pride and accomplishment. His moment of vindication had come; his foe was defeated, and the glory of his house would be restored. He thought of his old command, the *Bortas;* it would not be long before her deck would be beneath his feet once more.

"Cease firing," he ordered at last. "Prepare a boarding party." Raising his voice in victory, he bellowed words he had long yearned to say. "Bring me Archer!"

As if in reply, a nearby console issued a shrill alarm. His first officer glanced down at once, then raised his startled gaze to meet Duras's.

"Three ships approaching!"

The image coalesced on the viewscreen: three ships,

indeed. Duras's lips twisted as he gnashed his ragged teeth at the sight.

The screen filled with blinding light; the bird-of-prey convulsed under the attack.

"Earth vessels!" the first officer shouted.

Duras was filled with venom; so great was his hatred that, had he been able to reach out into space and pommel the vessels with his own hands, he would have. How dare they interfere now, when victory was so close! "Return fire!" he roared.

But the bird-of-prey was no match for the relentless fire of three ships. The bridge began to shake as if it were trying to tear itself apart; Duras lifted a hand to shield himself from the rain of sparks as first one, then two consoles exploded.

"Shields are failing!" the tactical officer called.

The ship reeled; Duras held on to the arms of his chair as he responded, "Are they offline?"

"No, sir."

"Then keep firing!" Duras insisted. He had not come this far to give up so easily.

The bird-of-prey continued to vibrate so fiercely that Duras's teeth chattered; the vessel began to groan like a wounded *targ*.

The first officer turned to direct a meaningful stare at Duras. "We've lost disruptor banks three and four!"

In other words, the ship had no way of protecting herself or continuing the attack.

For an instant, fury so blinded Duras he could not see

his first officer's face, or the viewscreen beyond, where the Earth ships continued firing. His warrior's heart yearned to stay, to do whatever desperate act necessary to capture Archer. . . .

And yet, his mind was forced to admit that there *was* no way to capture Archer. Not now, at least. He was forced once again to bide his time.

Duras slammed his fist so hard against a console that the metal was dented.

"Withdraw," he growled, bitter. "Go to warp speed!"

On the bridge of the *Enterprise*, Archer struggled to sort out an odd mix of emotions: relief that Duras had called off his attack and disappeared, gratitude that Earth ships had come to his aid, and both gladness and sorrow to be home.

"It's Captain Ramirez, sir," Hoshi announced from her console. "On the *Intrepid*."

Archer nodded.

A new image appeared on the viewscreen—that of Carlos Ramirez, a captain in Starfleet and an acquaintance of Archer's. Carlos was, like Archer, in his early forties, a fit, olive-skinned man with smooth dark hair. At the moment, his lips curled upwards in a genuine smile, revealing small, even teeth.

"Captain Archer . . ."

Archer smiled faintly, and replied, his tone grateful. "It's good to see you, Carlos."

"What the hell was that all about?" Ramirez asked, referring to the encounter with the bird-of-prey.

Archer shrugged. "A Klingon named Duras . . . He's not very fond of me." Nor, Archer reflected, was he particularly fond of Duras at the moment. The Klingon had tried several times to kill him . . . and was responsible for having Archer's advocate, an old Klingon lawyer named Kolos, sent to Rura Penthe, the unspeakably brutal penal colony. Kolos had actually been a compassionate, decent sort, interested in helping Archer—but had paid for his concern. Archer wondered whether the old Klingon was still alive.

"Welcome home, Captain," Ramirez said, drawing Archer from his reverie. "I wish it was under better circumstances."

The first time Archer had seen Earth from low orbit, he'd thought it the most beautiful sight he'd ever seen: now it was one of the most painful.

As much he hadn't wanted to direct the *Enterprise* to hover over the area of the attack, it was impossible—as impossible as staying away from a loved one's funeral. Mayweather had silently guided the ship to the coordinates, and now, Florida and Cuba filled the bridge viewscreen.

The peninsula and island were still green, as Archer remembered, lightly obscured here and there by wisps of clouds, and the Gulf of Mexico a turquoise blue . . . But a series of long, black, diagonal lines strafed both land and water. *Each one several miles wide,* Admiral Forrest had said. *'Fire from the sky,'* survivors called it. *It just incinerated everything in its path, leaving lifeless craters behind.*

Not a word was spoken—but Archer managed a surreptitious glance at Trip Tucker. He remembered when he'd first met Trip. Tucker had been grinning then, full of fun and looking for trouble.

Now the engineer's eyes were narrowed, his lips taut with grief . . . and something which troubled the Captain even more: hatred, and a desire for revenge.

It was night in San Francisco, cool and damp. As the fog rolled in off the Bay, Archer felt a sense of relief that Starfleet Headquarters looked pretty much the same as the last time he'd seen it. It was a reassuring reminder that most residents of Earth were still intact, still going about their usual business.

And yet it was impossible to deny that what had happened had changed everyone and everything.

Certainly it had affected Admiral Forrest severely. Flanked by the Vulcan ambassador, Soval, Forrest stood in his office looking haggard. His black uniform only served to emphasize the fact that his face was now as ashen as his close-cropped hair; beneath his gray brows, his eyes were limned with dark shadows. Despite the urgency of his words, his tone revealed his weariness. "I told Command every word you said. They're having a hard time buying it."

Frustration coursed through Archer. He did not like having to believe Silik's mysterious master, either, but he did not see where they had a choice. "Do they have a better idea of who did this?"

Forrest didn't even try to reply.

Archer turned on Soval. The ambassador was, as always, maddeningly calm and composed in his green Vulcan robes and black cape; there was, in his detachment, a hint of disdain. He, like Forrest, was also silver-haired, but probably a century or two older. There was something in Soval's polished mannerisms that reminded Archer uncomfortably of Silik. In fact, at the moment, Archer was beginning to think that he liked the Suliban better.

Soval's eyes were scarcely open, his hands steepled, as if he were in meditation; he faced serenely forward, meeting no one's gaze, while Archer paced about.

"And how about the Vulcans?" the Captain said, less than politely. "I suppose you think I'm hallucinating?"

Soval did not deny the charge. "Our Science Directorate has determined that time travel is impossible."

Archer leaned closer to both men, his manner fiercely intent. "Are you all willing to risk a second attack?"

Neither replied.

"All I'm asking is to take *Enterprise* and find these Xindi. What do we have to lose, a single starship? Seems like a small price to pay if there's one chance in a million he was right."

Soval was unmoved. "Do you know where these coordinates he gave you are?" His tone made it clear that he already knew the answer.

Archer played along. "At warp five . . . about a three-month trip."

"They're inside the Delphic Expanse," Soval said, as if Archer should find this extremely meaningful.

Archer didn't. "What's that?"

"A region of space nearly a thousand light-years across. Vulcan ships have entered it . . . but only a few have returned."

Now it was Archer's turn to react with disdain. "You sound like you're talking about the Bermuda Triangle." He wondered whether the area still existed after the alien attack.

"There have been reports of fierce and dangerous species," Soval continued gravely, "unexplained anomalies. . . . In some regions, even the laws of physics don't apply." He paused and at last, faced Archer and held his gaze. "Twenty years ago, a Klingon vessel emerged from the Expanse. Every crewman on board was anatomically inverted, their bodies splayed open. And they were still alive."

Archer could not keep from wincing inwardly at the image—but outwardly, he refused to show that Soval's words had any effect on him.

The Vulcan finished. "You'd be more than foolish to pursue this course of action."

Archer responded by completely ignoring the Ambassador and turning instead to Forrest. "It's a risk I'm willing to take . . . and I imagine most of my crew would be with me."

"This is typical of your impulsiveness," Soval said, his uninflected tone belying the sharply critical nature of his words. "You'd be putting your crew's lives at stake when you have no evidence that anything you were told was true."

Archer kept his gaze fixed on the Admiral. It was clear that Forrest had heard him—and was seriously considering his point of view—but was still unconvinced.

At last, Forrest sighed, then spoke. "We've lost a lot of people already, Jon. Starfleet Command would need . . . some kind of proof before they'd let you go."

"I'm not sure if the person I spoke to was from the future or not," Archer countered, "but he knew that this would be the reaction I'd get . . ." he paused. "So he *did* give me proof."

He felt a small glimmer of satisfaction of the look of surprise on Forrest's—and quite possibly Soval's—face.

Admiral Forrest led them both to the hangar where Starfleet had stored the remnants of the alien probe; a nod from the Admiral permitted them to pass two security guards without incident.

The hangar was shrouded in shadow, save for the bright lights that illuminated the area where the wreckage was heaped, and the small refrigerated unit that housed the alien pilot's remains.

Archer stepped up to a large, jagged piece of scorched, twisted metal, adorned with tendrils of alien circuitry. He withdrew a scanner from his pocket and, with a deep intake of breath and a sincere wish that Silik had not once again played him for a fool, touched the controls on the scanner.

"Jon?" Forrest asked, his tone curious.

"This is quantum data from the debris." The scanner beeped; Archer held it so that both he and Forrest could read the results. "Take a look."

Forrest did.

"The principal alloy in this piece was synthesized within the last four years," Archer said, trying not to be disappointed. He moved to another section of debris and scanned it.

"*This* one, about a year earlier . . ."

Soval spoke, with less-than-perfect Vulcan patience. "What exactly are you trying to show us, Captain?"

Archer took pleasure in ignoring him—while at the same time growing more impatient himself. If Silik's master had been lying after all . . . He moved to yet another section, and performed yet another scan.

"Twelve years for this piece . . ."

Even Forrest was becoming slightly annoyed. "Your point, Jonathan?"

"I'm getting to it," Archer said, a little desperately. He looked around, trying to find a scrap of metal, a piece of debris, clearly different from the rest. He lifted up a chunk of metal and peered underneath.

And there he saw it: an intact piece of machinery—or perhaps, more accurately, technology—the size of his fist. He took it in his hand and scanned it, then checked the readout.

He turned to Admiral Forrest with a sense of triumph and held out the scanner. "You might find this interesting."

Forrest glanced at the readout—did a beautiful double-take, then stared at it again. "Your scanner's not working properly."

"Why's that, sir?" Archer was careful to keep any hint of gloating from his tone.

"The quantum reads *minus* four-twenty."

"And what's wrong with that?" Archer was fishing and enjoying it.

"Quantum always registers in positive numbers," Forrest stated, his tone dismissive.

But Archer had come prepared. He pulled a second scanner from his pocket and held it up to the alien component. "Then I guess this one's not working, either." He didn't show it, but he felt an enormous surge of relief and vindication. Silik's master had been telling the truth after all. And he would not have intervened if there hadn't been a good chance that a second attack could be stopped.

He had contacted Archer—which meant that it was up to the captain to do something about it—and nothing could stop Archer now, not Soval, not Admiral Forrest, not even Starfleet Command. He'd already made up his mind to find a way to stop the Xindi, even if it meant disobeying orders.

Despite Ambassador Soval's apparent disinterest, the Vulcan could no longer ignore what was happening. He strode up to Archer, took the scanner, and regarded the readout with distaste.

"You said he told you this 'faction from the future' "—

the ambassador uttered the words with a skepticism that far exceeded T'Pol's—"could only *communicate* through time." He looked up at Archer, his brows lifted slightly, an expression of Vulcan disbelief. "So how do you suggest they got this component to the Xindi?"

Archer faced him fiercely. Soval seemed to have already made up his mind—regardless of how "logical" the evidence was. "I haven't the slightest idea. But that doesn't change what's on that scanner." He nodded at the component from the Xindi ship. "That fragment's from the future. Unless you have another explanation."

The Ambassador was unmoved. "The 'lack of another explanation' doesn't make your assumption correct."

Archer gave up on him: Clearly, the Vulcans were too deeply mired in their dogma concerning time travel to be persuaded. Instead, the Captain turned his focus on Admiral Forrest.

And in Forrest's weary eyes, there shone the first stirring of belief. Archer felt a surge of victory, even before the Admiral said quietly:

"I'll speak with Command."

Soval shook his head in suspiciously humanlike disapproval and frustration.

Archer took pleasure in ignoring him, and gestured at the morgue unit. If Starfleet gave the *Enterprise* permission, Archer would need to be able to recognize the enemy he would be dealing with. "I'd like to take a look in there," he said grimly.

Forrest nodded to the nearby security guards; one

49

came forward and worked a control console next to the unit.

The covering slid open, releasing a blast of cold vapor that turned to mist in the warmer air.

Archer looked down through the white swirls; beneath lay the scorched, battered remains of the probe's pilot.

The Captain was not quiet sure what he had expected to see—perhaps a hairless race, sleek and exotic, like the Suliban, futuristic-looking. Instead, what he saw was the charred corpse of a tall biped, dressed in twisted remnants of metallic armor. The creature's face was so badly scorched its features had caved inward, making any guesses as to its actual appearance impossible.

The Captain raised his scanner over the alien corpse.

"Are you suggesting this is a Xindi?" Soval's tone was still laced with skepticism.

Archer didn't even glance up. "I sure as hell would like to find out."

Chapter 5

Archer returned to the *Enterprise*, still in orbit around Earth, and found a summons from Phlox awaiting him. He proceeded immediately to sickbay, where he found the doctor in the company of a stern-looking Vulcan.

Phlox's usual abundantly cheerful manner was subdued—in part because of the tragedy which had occurred on Earth. But at least part of it was due to his visitor; Archer got the strange impression that the Denobulan, who was always avidly friendly and interested in everyone and everything, didn't much care for the Vulcan.

Even so, Phlox's tone was pleasant. "This is Doctor Fer'at."

Fer'at was slight, with hair the color of steel and a jumpsuit to match; his eyes were large and probing.

Archer scowled at him impatiently. "I don't have a lot of time. What's up?"

Phlox answered in Fer'at's stead. "The Vulcan research team detected traces of pyritic radiation in the alien debris."

"Why didn't Starfleet catch it?" Archer asked.

"Some of our technology is still more advanced than yours," Fer'at replied smoothly.

Archer's frown deepened; he'd had more than enough of Vulcans and their patronizing attitudes.

Phlox sensed the Captain's irritation and leaned forward, his tone mollifying. "We're going to need to treat anyone who got close to the wreckage. Doctor Fer'at is here to determine the extent of your exposure."

Fer'at motioned to a nearby diagnostic bed. "It shouldn't take long," he told Archer. "Please sit down."

Archer sat grudgingly. The Vulcan produced a type of medical scanner the Captain had never seen before, and began to wave it over Archer's body. Meanwhile, Phlox moved to a nearby console and continued some work of his own.

Fer'at assumed a clinical air. "Have you experienced any nausea or dizziness?"

"No." Archer was still puzzling over the fact that Starfleet had failed to detect the radiation. He couldn't afford to have something like this cause problems; certainly, the time traveler would have warned him if the radiation posed a danger . . .

"Numbness in your extremeties?" Fer'at queried.

"I feel fine," Archer said.

Fer'at was silent for a moment as he checked his scanner's readout, then continued working. "I was told you think a piece of the wreckage came from the future."

Archer glared at him with frank annoyance. "I know. Vulcans don't believe in time travel."

"Some of us do," Fer'at replied simply.

That threw the Captain for a loop; he blinked, disbelieving.

"Tell me," Fer'at continued, with sudden interest, "this 'time traveler' you met, was he humanoid?"

"How do you know about that?"

Fer'at gave a small shrug. "I was briefed before coming here."

"He seemed humanoid," Archer answered, intrigued that a Vulcan might actually be convinced of the truth. "I couldn't see him that well."

"Have you encountered people from the future before?"

"A number of times," Archer said. He paused; there was something suspicious about Fer'at and his curiosity, about his whole story. And he had never known a Vulcan so eager to make small talk. "Does this have anything to do with the radiation?"

"I'm just curious," Fer'at countered mildly. He stepped behind the Captain and began to scan his back. "It must be difficult to have so many people question your story. Does it upset you?"

"It doesn't help." Archer's tone was cold.

"But how does it make you feel?"

That was it—Archer had had it with Fer'at and his examination. From between gritted teeth, he replied, not at all nicely, "I told you, it doesn't help." From his peripheral vision, he could see Phlox stop working and gaze piercingly at the Vulcan; obviously, the doctor was also becoming suspicious. Archer watched as Phlox began to tap some controls.

Fer'at blinked his large, slightly protruding eyes. "I can sense some anger when you talk about this . . ."

Sense? What was there to "sense" when Archer was purposely letting it show? His words clipped, the Captain replied, "It's kind of strange that a Vulcan would be so interested in my 'feelings.' "

"Just curious." Fer'at echoed his previous statement. He continued to scan, then consulted the readout for a moment before stating, "Your exposure seems minimal . . . You'll require very little treatment." He directed his probing stare back to Archer. "I imagine you must have felt very anxious after meeting someone from the future."

Archer's tone was blatantly sarcastic. "Why would you imagine that?"

He was on the verge of rising from the bed and ordering the Vulcan out when Phlox intervened. The Denobulan's voice was filled with outrage; Archer was taken aback by the normally placid doctor's anger.

"I'm afraid this 'examination' is over."

"I'm nearly finished," Fer'at replied calmly.

"You *are* finished," Phlox said unequivocally. He turned to Archer. "I just checked the Vulcan database. There's only one Doctor Fer'at listed, and he's not a pathologist . . . He's a psychiatric analyst."

Archer pushed himself from the bed. According to T'Pol, Vulcans prided themselves on their honesty—but Soval was just one of the most underhanded, deceitful people Archer'd ever met. He turned on Fer'at with fury. "Soval sure is persistent. What did he want you to do, come back with proof that I'm out of my mind?"

Phlox was as angry as Archer had ever seen him; the Denobulan's ridged brow was knit together in an intimidating scowl. "You come to my sickbay under false pretenses! Where are your medical ethics!"

Fer'at remained calm and uncowed. "I'm just doing what I was told to do."

"Well, *I'm* telling you to get the hell off my ship!" Archer said, with more than a little satisfaction. He turned to the doctor. "If you don't mind, Phlox, I'd like you to escort our guest to the airlock."

"Gladly," Phlox said, and led the Vulcan away with an air of righteous indignation.

The pale blue Florida sky was filled with the fat cumulus clouds of summer, some of them edged an ominous charcoal, reminding Trip of the pending afternoon rainshower. They had time yet, he knew. Give it two, three hours, and the skies would open: for half an hour, sheets of water would slam down, soaking and cooling the heated earth . . . then it would all be over, and the clouds would disappear, as if nothing had happened.

At the moment, Trip stood beside Reed on a hillside. Florida, of course, had no hills (save for a very few)—the

peninsula was unrelentingly flat, allowing an unob-
structed view for miles. The first time Trip had visited
mountains, he'd felt closed in, claustrophobic, seasick as
a landlubber.

At least, Florida *hadn't* had any hillsides—until now.

Trip stared down dully into the black, miles-wide
crater that separated the remaining half of his hometown
from the other. Normally, the smell of the sea and the
chatter of gulls had a tonic, calming effect on him—but
today, the ocean smell was overlaid by the smell of
scorched rubble, and the call of birds drowned out by the
sound of reconstruction crews. Trip's insides felt like the
wounded land—gouged open, laid bare.

Across the chasm, tall palms still swayed in the sub-
tropical breeze; tiny workers moved in and around the
remains, while half-demolished buildings still smol-
dered. Overhead, shuttlepods sailed beneath the
clouds. *Looky-loos*, Trip thought bitterly, then realized
that he was wrong. Starfleet had cordoned off this air-
space to all but essential personnel, locals, and family
members. Trip had had to prove his next-of-kin status
in order to be permitted to visit the restricted area—
and it'd been hard enough to get permission for Reed
to accompany him.

Neither he nor Reed spoke for a full minute after set-
ting down; the scene was too horrific, too awesome in
scope to permit anything beyond silent contemplation.
This was, after all, a vast graveyard, a memorial to the
dead. And not just human: *every* life-form here had per-

ished, both plant and animal, including a great deal of ocean life. Lizzie would have regretted that, too; she loved the sea as much as her brother.

After a time, Malcolm said softly, "I'm so sorry. . . ."

Trip couldn't respond right away. The danger of choking up was too great. Instead, he tried to distract himself by orienting himself to the surroundings, recreating the missing town in his memory.

He pointed to a location inside the crater and felt a stab of pain. "The house was over there . . . less than a kilometer."

That prompted an immediate barrage of unuttered questions: Had Lizzie been inside, working, when the horror had occurred? Had she been in town, running errands? Had she run outside at the sound of devastation and seen the blast headed towards her? Had she had time to realize what was happening, or did it—please— happen too quickly for her to know anything, feel anything?

Or had she been scared? Had she felt pain?

Stop it, Trip told himself firmly. First off, Lizzie was tough and pragmatic; she would have faced death matter- of-factly, so there was no point in tormenting himself. Yet he couldn't seem to keep his mind from going over every possible scenario, including the one suggested by the Captain—that Lizzie had gone out of town, that she was okay. But Trip knew his sister too well: she was utterly responsible, and would have contacted him immediately.

She knew how her big brother worried about her, despite the fact that she was perfectly capable of taking care of herself.

So Trip had gone through the tedious process of locating a neighbor who knew Lizzie, who might have known whether she'd been in town that day.

It'd been hell finding someone who was still alive—the list of casualties was heartrending, including scores of families Trip had known from childhood. He'd finally tracked down the owner of the Seafood Shanty, where Liz was a regular, who said he'd thought he'd seen her in town that morning. But the trauma had left his memory uncertain.

Thought he'd seen her. That would have to do; that, and Lizzie's silence. So much for closure.

Trip found himself starting to tear up, and distracted himself again by searching for a landmark. To his delight, he found one—on the other side of the miles-wide swath of destruction. The sight almost made him smile; not everything from his early years had vanished into oblivion.

"See that building?" He pointed again; Reed's gaze followed the gesture. "The white one . . . it was a movie theater . . ." He let go a short, unhappy laugh. "When we were kids, if I didn't take my sister with me, she'd scream like a banshee. . . ." He paused, allowing himself a happy memory, of himself and Lizzie munching popcorn in the very first row, heads tilted back so far their necks ached, their eyes saucer-wide. "I can't tell you how many movies we saw there. . . ."

Reed nodded. As much as the two men ribbed each other and often argued, Reed had proven himself a true friend. It was he who suggested in the most delicate way that he would be honored to go with Tucker to see the attack site. *Best,* Reed had said, *to see for yourself, to answer your own questions. Sometimes that's easier than leaving things to your imagination . . .* Malcolm spoke, his tone gentle, tentative.

"Are you certain she was here when this happened?"

Trip's expression and tone darkened. "Someone would've heard from her if she wasn't." *Especially me . . .*

The sight of the scorched terrain was all Trip would ever have for proof. He forced himself to accept that, but there was one thing he could never accept: the fact that an entire race of beings were evil enough to have done such a thing . . . and, according to the captain, they planned to do it again.

Trip's heart was scarred, blackened by hatred. Maybe these beings had a good reason for what they did; maybe the answer lay in diplomacy, not war.

But at the moment, he didn't care. He *wanted* bloodshed, wanted revenge.

Someone had to pay for what had happened to Lizzie.

Captain's Starlog, supplemental. After days of debate, Starfleet's finally informed me that we're to proceed with our new mission.

Archer was far above the damage site, seated shoulder-to-shoulder beside Admiral Forrest in the cramped cockpit of an inspection pod. The two were maneuvering around the spacedock where the skeleton of a new star-ship was being constructed.

The Captain had felt a deep sense of relief on receiving permission to head for the Expanse; he'd been determined to go anyway, and having official sanction made things much easier. At the same time, he felt a sense of exhilaration that was not precisely pleasant. These were far more dangerous circumstances than the ones surrounding the *Enterprise's* first sally into space.

Archer looked on the vessel with admiration and a bit of envy. "The NX-02 . . ."

"She'll be ready to launch in fourteen months," Forrest said, with no small amount of pride.

"A long time," Archer said. Currently, he had serious doubts about whether he'd be alive to step aboard her.

Forrest's hearty, encouraging tone rang a bit false. "Hopefully, you'll be back well before then."

"Hopefully," Archer replied, without enthusiasm. He changed the subject. "What kind of armaments will she have?"

"The same complement of weapons you'll have when the retrofit is done." He paused. "Have you told your crew?"

"This morning."

"How many are staying aboard?"

It wasn't an easy subject for Archer to consider. On one hand, he wanted and needed each and every crew member; at the same time, he dreaded asking them to accompany him on such a perilous mission. He was all too aware that he bore the responsibility for each of their lives, and so he had been careful not to pressure any of them, but simply to give them the facts and let them come to their own decisions.

"Some haven't decided yet," he answered Forrest at last, "but I don't think more than eight or nine will be leaving." After a pause, he added, "I talked to General Casey a few hours ago."

The admiral nodded. "His team should be arriving at eighteen hundred hours." He directed a sidewise glance at Archer, one silver eyebrow lifted. "I'm surprised you asked for them. You think you'll be comfortable with military on board?"

Archer shrugged casually, even though he had in fact *not* been comfortable with the idea at first—but it had seemed the best thing for the mission, and so he had reconciled himself to it. "T'Pol and Phlox have worked out pretty well," he said. "I don't have a problem with non-Starfleet personnel." He turned his face toward Forrest's. "The General tells me these are the best he has. I'm going to need all the muscle I can get when we cross into the Expanse."

The very utterance of the word *Expanse* made a muscle in the Admiral's jaw spasm. Archer understood exactly how his superior felt; Forrest bore the same sense of responsibility for the lives of those aboard *Enterprise* as Archer did. "You weren't told *where* in this Expanse you're supposed to look?"

"Not even a hint," Archer answered honestly.

"And this weapon they're building . . . did he say how long it was going to take them?"

The Captain didn't answer the question directly. "I don't think he would've warned us if we didn't have a chance of stopping them."

Forrest's tone suddenly grew heated. "If he knows where these Xindi are, why the hell won't he tell you?"

The same notion had occurred to Archer; he couldn't blame the Admiral for his frustration. He also couldn't answer his question.

Forrest drew in an exasperated breath, then said at last, "I guess it's time to head back." He glanced at Archer. "You want to join us for dinner?"

"Thanks," Archer replied, "but I've got plans." And that was the first and only thing that made him genuinely, inwardly smile, for the first time in days.

A few hours later, Archer pulled his jacket closed against the chill of the San Francisco night. It was nostalgic to be in the city again, walking down the narrow, brightly lit streets of Chinatown. Only one thing was different: the streets seemed emptier; he passed only a few people on his way to the restaurant.

At last he found his way to the old-fashioned glass doors of The Lotus Blossom Restaurant; the very sight made him smile faintly. As he opened the door and stepped in, the sight of the maître d'—a diminuitive Asian man, nattily dressed in a business suit and tie— made his smile grow broader.

"You're a sight for sore eyes, Tommy," Archer said warmly. It'd been a couple of years, but Tommy hadn't changed an iota.

"Jonathan." The maître d' flashed him a grin.

Archer looked around. It was the weekend, and normally, there'd have been a line of hungry patrons snaking all the way out the door . . . but on this night, he counted lots of empty tables. "Slow tonight."

Tommy's grin faded at once. "People are staying home . . . ever since . . ."

He didn't need to say any more; Archer understood at once. He'd actually allowed himself to view the local news briefly, before coming here; the media were incessant in their coverage of the tragedy, even though they had no more real information to give. Now they were speculating about future attacks—and they didn't seem to see the connection between that and the other news story Archer had caught, that people were afraid, and staying home with their families.

He could understand; if he'd had a home and a kitchen, he'd want to be there, too.

"She here?" he asked Tommy.

The maître d' pointed. "Over there." His tone became at once scolding and teasing. "You're late."

Archer smiled again. "Thanks. Bring me a Scotch."

"Right away."

Tommy headed for the bar, while Archer moved toward the indicated table.

He failed to notice his surroundings—failed to notice

his own posture, his expression, whether he smiled or
not in greeting. All Archer noticed was that he was suddenly seated across from a woman, who delicately swallowed a bit of the half-eaten appetizer in front of her.

Rebecca. She was wearing her hair differently; it had
grown out a bit, and was shoulder-length now, parted on
one side, and it seemed to have more of a reddish cast to
it. But her eyes were still luminous pale green, her face
still handsome. She wore a lowcut lavender shirt that
suited her coloring perfectly.

"I'm really sorry," Archer said, and she smiled
whimsically at that. It was as though he had just left
room for a short while, as if he hadn't been away for a
year, as if they had just had dinner together the night
before.

"I can't remember the last time you *weren't* late," she
said with dry good humor. Her tone changed abruptly,
became somber. "Did they bring you back because of
what happened?"

Archer looked down at the tablecloth. He didn't have
to answer; Rebecca understood, as she almost always
did, without words.

"For how long?" she asked.

"I wish it was longer . . ." Archer said honestly. "I was
hoping to spend some time with you."

Tommy appeared silently and smoothly, without interrupting the flow of the conversation, set the Scotch in
front of him. He took a long drink.

"How's Porthos?" she asked. She always inquired after

the beagle; it was her mother, after all, who'd given Archer the dog from one of her prize litters. Four fine males; four little Musketeers, she'd called them, and that'd been that. The rowdy little pup had been christened on the spot.

"He's great," Archer said, reminded that despite the horror of the past several days, there were still good things in life. Porthos was one of them—unconnected to the tragedy, unaware of it, always happy to see his master. "Turns out he loves space—if he even realizes he's out there. He's a trouper."

She smiled faintly at that; another long silence ensued, during which time her expression grew grim.

"Do they know who did this?" Rebecca asked him. "*Why* they did this?"

"We know a little bit, but not enough." He smiled apologetically and shook his head as he picked up his chopsticks and stole a bite of her dinner. "I'll probably be gone for a long time, Becky."

As always, she refused to be sentimental. "You've been gone for a long time before."

He set down the chopsticks and permitted himself to look at her—really *look* at her, to memorize her as she was now. And he could see at once that she understood, in typical lightning-Rebecca-fashion, that he was not talking about a typical mission.

She tried at once to lighten the mood. "If I find out you've got a girl in every spaceport . . ."

He smiled and reached across the table to take her

face in his hands; he had forgotten the warmth, the softness of her skin, and impulsively leaned across the table and kissed her, gently.

Rebecca was not one to be outdone; she returned the kiss, full force, and when at last they broke from each other, both were breathing audibly.

"I suppose you expect me to invite you back to my apartment," she said wryly.

Archer kept his tone light. "What are my chances?"

She picked up a fortune cookie from a small plate and opened it with a resounding crack, then pulled out the small strip of paper hidden inside. She read it studiously, puckering her brow, then glanced back up at him.

"You're in luck . . ."

Chapter 6

Aboard the *Enterprise,* T'Pol entered sickbay tentatively.

It was not her habit to solicit advice from others, or to discuss personal decisions; logic generally dictated an obvious path.

But in this case, logic failed, and meditation did little to clarify the issue. T'Pol knew what her instincts told her—to remain on board, to continue serving with the crew. She would be needed for the difficult journey ahead.

Instincts, however, were often tainted with emotion, and T'Pol could not permit feeling to influence such a critical decision. Ethically, she was bound to follow the dictates of the Vulcan High Command, and remain behind. She had an influential career as a diplomat awaiting her; to risk entering the Expanse was to risk years of training. It was not easy for the High Command to locate Vulcans willing to work closely with humans, and T'Pol was not only willing, she had become comfortable in their company. That made her a valuable commodity to the Vulcan government. As willing as she might be to sacrifice her own life because it could possibly help save the human race, she had to think of the impact her choice would have on her own people.

She entered sickbay in search of clarity.

The physician Phlox was seated at his work station, peering at the screen. Even in repose, his round, ridged face radiated benevolence. Although she had studied them, T'Pol had never met any other members of his species; she suspected Phlox would be considered somewhat eccentric even by Denobulan standards. He wore no uniform, instead preferring to drape himself in colorful tunics, and his passion for unusual, even bizarre, forms of medical treatment had become legendary throughout Starfleet.

Despite his unique personality, however, and the fact that Denobulans were at least as emotional as humans, T'Pol had come to find that Phlox was actually quite clear-headed and pragmatic; he had a talent for sifting through a number of complicated factors and making the right choice, perhaps the result of his being a skilled diagnostician. He was also strongly intuitive—a trait T'Pol's people distrusted, and yet Phlox's intuition generally resulted in his coming to a sound conclusion.

Phlox sensed her presence immediately, and looked over at her. "Sub-Commander? Is there something I can do for you?"

T'Pol wasted no time; there was no point in pretending, for dignity's sake, that she had come here for anything other than advice. She trusted Phlox's integrity and discretion utterly; he would not repeat their conversation to any other member of the crew. "Are you confident with your decision, Doctor?"

He swiveled in his chair to face her fully. "What decision would that be?"

"To remain on *Enterprise*," T'Pol said. To explain how she had deduced the fact, she said, "Crewman Fuller just told me a shuttle is on its way with two hundred snow beetles."

The Denobulan's expression grew coy. "They could be for my replacement."

"There isn't a doctor in Starfleet who would have the slightest idea of what to do with them," T'Pol countered drily.

Phlox grinned brightly, acknowledging the fact with good humor and even a tinge of pride. He grew a bit more somber, then pressed, "And what about you?"

T'Pol hesitated. Rather than address her conflict directly, she said, "The High Council has made it clear that they don't want me to enter the Delphic Expanse."

Phlox's manner grew pointed. "I'm more interested in hearing what *you* want."

His words unsettled her; surely he understood that this issue was far too important for personal desires to interfere. "It's not my place to disobey the High Command."

"Nonsense," the doctor contradicted her flatly. "You've done it before."

That silenced her. He was correct, of course. But she'd had good reason to do so then. . . .

"It's interesting, you and I," Phlox continued. "The only two aliens on board the vessel. To go, or to stay?" He paused, letting the question hang for a moment in the air. "For me, it was a simple question of loyalty toward the Captain . . . and the sad realization that he'll need me more than ever on such a crucial mission.

"But for *you*, it's a more difficult decision. Does your allegiance lie with the High Command, or with Captain Archer?"

Loyalty, T'Pol realized: that was indeed the crux of the issue. Loyalty, considered next to logic the highest of all Vulcan virtues. Should she remain loyal to the Captain she had served, who needed her now—or loyal to the bureaucracy who had forged her education, who might profit from her future career?

Once again, Phlox's insight proved remarkable.

The moment was interrupted by a crewman, who entered pushing a large, ventilated crate; from within came hundreds of soft chirps.

Phlox cocked his head and graced T'Pol with one of his impossible Denobulan smiles, the corners of his mouth quirking up sharply, far higher than human or Vulcan facial muscles could ever manage.

"Thank you," T'Pol said quietly. It was not her custom to express gratitude lightly; on Vulcan, it was not done at all. She had learned, as a student of diplomacy, that the act was highly important to humans, but she had always felt awkward doing it.

Now, she did not feel awkward at all; she was sincerely

grateful to the doctor for helping her make what would no doubt prove to be the most important decision of her life.

She exited sickbay, leaving Phlox behind to chirp happily at his new tenants.

Inside her quarters, Hoshi Sato was busy packing. That act filled her with a strange nostalgia: there were a lot of things she was leaving behind, a lot of things she would no longer need.

On her bed lay a pile of civvies, neatly folded and ready to be packed into a nearby container—her mother had chided her over the fact that they were not only worn out, but out of style, so they were going back to be recycled. At the moment, she was going through her bookshelves, trying to decide which ones she could bear to part with. It wasn't easy, but she decided to be tough.

She ran her hand over a volume: *An Introduction to Farsi, Volumes I–III*. It was well written, with wonderful tidbits about the culture; she hated to leave it, but she'd already read through it twice, and had a working knowledge of the language.

Into the crate it went.

She picked up another one: *Advanced Attic Greek*. A bit pedantic, but still a good read. She sighed; it would have to go, too. Into the crate.

The door chimed; she turned to face it. "Come in."

Archer entered, looking a bit more rested, a bit less tense than he'd been in previous days.

"What a pleasant surprise," Hoshi said.

Archer smiled. "How'd it go with your folks?" There was something sad, poignant in the smile that made Hoshi want to make him feel better. They'd all been moved by the tragedy, but now it was time to get on with the mission. Hoshi herself felt the need to streamline her cabin, to get rid of everything extraneous. Besides, it helped ease her nervous anticipation until the mission got under way.

Her tone was light, teasing. "I think I might need to brush up on my Japanese."

Archer sat on the edge of the bed, careful not to disturb the containers, and let go a barely audible snicker. "I doubt it."

Hoshi continued to pack, comfortable in the Captain's presence, although uncertain as to why he had come.

"We got new upgrades for the Universal Translator," Archer said.

She was pleased. "That ought to make life a lot easier." She'd been more than a little concerned about the types of alien languages they were going to encounter.

"It'll never replace a linguist with a magical ear," Archer said.

Was it her imagination, or was his voice a bit husky? She smiled. "Not so magical." She went back to her packing, pulling another book from the shelf.

"That's a matter of opinion." The Captain paused. "You've been invaluable to this mission . . . to *me* . . . ever since we left spacedock. You were a little shaky at first . . . but who wasn't?"

Hoshi was touched; rather than reply—she didn't quite know what to say to such kind words—she glanced down at the open book in her hands, closed it, and put it back on the shelf.

Curious, Archer retrieved it, and peered at the cover.

"Languages of the Sub-Sahara," he read, then said, with humor, "I'm surprised you're leaving this one here."

Hoshi didn't get the joke. She looked at him blankly and said, "I haven't read it yet."

It was Archer's turn to be puzzled. "So why not take it with you?"

Hoshi stared at him for an instant—and suddenly understood. Archer was sad, and telling her what she'd meant to him, because he thought she was packing to *leave.* He thought he had been saying good-bye.

"Captain . . ." She pointed to the half-filled container. "I'm sending *these* books home to my mother. That'll give me more shelf space. There's been a lot written about alien languages since we've been gone."

Archer's expression was one of dawning relief. "And the clothes are going to . . ."

". . . to my mother." Hoshi gave a wry little grimace. "I thought it might be time to 'upgrade' my civvies."

A beat, then Archer admitted, "I thought you were leaving?"

Her tone was gently scolding. "Why would you think that?"

He shrugged. "I don't know . . . You're a teacher, an academic . . ."

"And that means I'm not capable of handling myself on the new mission?"

"That's not what I meant . . ."

She stopped packing and faced him, her manner adamant. "I don't know what's inside this Expanse, sir, but I think I've proven that I can handle myself in difficult situations . . . and even provide a little help along the way." She paused, searching his face. "I assume you have no problem with my remaining on board."

Archer smiled faintly; in his expression, she saw both sincere gladness that she was coming along—and deep concern over her safety.

"I wouldn't have it any other way," he said.

With Commander Tucker beside him, Malcolm Reed watched with keen interest as a quartet of crewmen wheeled in a weighed-down cart bearing four sleek, shining, and incalculably deadly torpedoes. The sight made Reed swell with an odd pride: *Enterprise* would now be better able to defend herself, no matter what she encountered.

The four crewmen were met by others, who helped lift the first of the heavy weapons and carefully insert them into the aperture of a freshly installed launch tube.

Reed felt a surge of satisfaction at the metallic sound of the torpedo sliding neatly into firing position. He turned to Trip Tucker.

"Photonic torpedoes," he said by way of explanation. Tucker had missed the briefing on the new weapons—

understandably, of course. "Their range is over fifty times greater than our conventional torpedoes."

Normally, Tucker would have been drooling over the sight of any new technology added to engineering or tactical. In fact, he would have been all over the torpedoes, asking rapid-fire, excited questions, insisting on helping the others to load them into the launch tubes, just so he could put his hands on him—but today, he merely stared with disinterest at the weapons and said nothing.

Concerned, Reed tried to provoke a reaction by providing further tempting details. "And they have variable yield. They can knock the com array off a shuttlepod without scratching the hull . . . or put a three-kilometer crater into an asteroid."

Tucker released a silent sigh and gazed briefly away, distracted. "How long's it gonna take to reconfigure the tubes?" Instead of being excited about the refit, he seemed bored and rather irritated by the fact that this would only waste more time. Reed understood; no doubt the Commander was eager to be under way, after so much time on Earth having nothing to do but think about the tragedy.

"We've got three teams working on it," Reed offered quickly. "They promise me it'll be done well before we leave spacedock. But I'm going to have to start integrating them into the power grid."

Tucker digested this in silence, then said curtly, "Let's go."

They moved out into the corridor, stepping around the

occasional crew member refitting a circuitry panel or bringing in new equipment.

Reed waited until they were out of anyone's earshot before bringing up a tender subject. It was one that had been troubling him for some weeks; he was beginning to worry that perhaps his friend needed help in dealing with his loss. Reed wanted to do something, but he had been lucky enough not to have experienced real grief; he had no idea what Trip might be going through, only that it was terribly difficult.

But he *did* know that it was best for a survivor to commemorate the death, to acknowledge it. Save for the single visit to Florida—a visit that had lasted only minutes before an overwhelmed Trip had to return to the ship—the Commander hadn't so much as mentioned his sister's name. And that, Reed knew, was not good.

He cleared his throat, then said delicately, "Is there going to be some kind of . . . service?"

Trip reacted swiftly, turning toward Reed as though he were a wasp who had just stung him. "For Lizzie?"

Reed nodded, silent.

Trip looked away and started walking faster; his lips pressed together so tightly they paled, and then he said, with barely restrained anger, "If you're talking about a funeral . . . it's kinda pointless when there's nothing left."

For his friend's sake, Reed persisted gently. "I guess I'm talking about a memorial."

Trip let go a dismissive huff of air. "My sister wasn't big on memorials."

"I read there was a day of remembrance for all the victims a couple of months ago. . . . I'm sorry you missed it." There; he'd said it. He had been worried about Tucker ever since the attack. The Commander had changed; instead of admitting his grief, and dealing with it, he instead refused to discuss it. But Reed could see the fury simmering inside him, growing stronger each day. At some point, the man was going to break.

In fact, Reed's words made Tucker furious; his tone rose. "Why are you so obsessed with memorials?"

"I'm not obsessed," Reed said mildly.

"She's dead." Tucker's voice was hoarse, flat, bitter. "So are seven million others. She was no more important than any of them."

Reed wasn't about to let him get away with such a statement. "She was more important to *you*. There's nothing wrong with admitting that."

He'd gone too far; it was more than Tucker could bear. He whirled about to face Reed, letting the rage show at last in his voice, his expression. "I'm getting real tired of you telling me what I can and can't do!" he shouted. "And while we're at it, I don't need you to remind me that Elizabeth was killed! So just let it alone!"

He paused, his face contorted, apparently waiting for a response; Reed, stunned into silence, gave him none.

"Maybe you should pay more attention to upgrading your weapons," Tucker snapped at last, "so you can blow the hell out of these bastards when we find them!"

He stalked off.

After a short pause, Reed drew a deep breath, then followed.

Inside Admiral Forrest's office, Archer sat at a conference table beside T'Pol across from Forrest and Soval. The summons had been evasive; Forrest's cryptic message had merely said that the Vulcan High Council wished to provide more information about the Expanse, and requested that both Archer and T'Pol come to Headquarters to view an entry from a ship's log.

Forrest seemed reluctant; obviously, the Vulcans had pressured him into this, without any regard for the fact that it was the middle of Earth's night.

Archer addressed his superior first. "With all due respect, Admiral, what's the point of me watching this?" He turned to the Vulcan Ambassador, who stood by with that damnably serene, superior manner of his. "Is it supposed to frighten me, make me change my mind about commanding this mission?"

As always, Soval didn't directly answer his question. "It's important for you to see what you'll be facing." The Vulcan turned toward a large wall monitor. "The *Vaankara* was in the Delphic Expanse for less than two days before we received a distress call." He paused. "This transmission arrived six hours later."

He tapped a control, causing the room to darken—then tapped another, and the screen brightened.

Clearly, the recording had been damaged: all the color had faded from it, registering the Vulcans on the bridge in black, white, and shades of gray. The images were jumpy, laced with static—but compelling nonetheless.

There came the sounds of a madhouse: of moans and screams, obscene utterances. The bridge was in chaos; bodies were in continuous motion. At first, Archer could make no sense of what was happening . . . and then he realized: the crew was *killing* each other bare-handed.

He stared, wanting to look away, as the second-in-command leapt for the elderly captain and clasped hands around his throat; there came the sound of bones crunching as the older man coughed up blood. Others at the helm wrestled each other to the floor.

At one point, the science officer viciously attacked another Vulcan, gouging his victim's eye out with a finger . . . then smearing the blood contentedly on his own cheek.

Archer looked away at last.

Blessedly, the screen dissolved into static; the lights came on.

"Less than an hour later," Soval said calmly, "the *Vaankara* was destroyed. There was no indication of a malfunction, or an attack."

"Are you suggesting the *crew* was responsible?" Archer asked.

Once again, Soval gave no direct answer. "I'm suggesting you reconsider this mission."

Archer let go a soft sound of pure exasperation. He had a job to do, and Soval no longer had any right to try to interfere. "That's not my decision to make," he said coldly, then turned and said, with respect, to Forrest, "Will there be anything else, sir?"

Forrest shook his head. He seemed reluctant to have yielded to Soval's pressure; at the same time, Archer understood why the Admiral had done it. It was only fair to let Archer know what he was getting into.

Flanked by T'Pol, Archer rose and moved to leave the room.

Behind them, Soval called, "I need to speak with you, T'Pol."

Archer swore silently at that. T'Pol was, quite simply, one of his most valuable crew members . . . and he had no doubt that Soval would do everything in his power to pressure her to stay. She would, of course; there was no reason for her to risk her life on behalf of Earth, and she had been put on *Enterprise* at the Ambassador's request, to keep the Vulcans informed of the mischief the humans were getting into.

That didn't make losing her any easier.

Outside the Fleet Operations Center, the night air was damp and chill. T'Pol found it bracing; she'd become accustomed to San Francisco weather during her time in the city as an intern. In addition, she had long ago adapted to the cooler temperatures aboard *Enterprise*. She supposed that if she returned to Vulcan, she'd have to reacclimate herself to the heat.

At the moment, she walked away from the Center past the large metal sculpture of Earth. Beside her was Soval, who wore his traditional heavy cloak to ward off the cold. T'Pol had yet to tell him of her desire to remain aboard *Enterprise*. She knew he would disapprove; she would have to word her case most carefully.

So she said nothing at first—merely listened, like a good diplomat.

Soval, of course, had already made plans without consulting her. T'Pol did not take offense; as her superior, he had a right.

"If all goes right," the Ambassador was saying, "you should be able to return to your duties on Earth within a year . . . that is, if you're still interested."

They made their way down the steps in front of the building.

If all goes well. What, precisely, was Soval saying? *If the taint of being around humans has sufficiently worn off . . . ? If you conduct yourself in an appropriate "Vulcan" manner for a long enough time . . . ?* She forced herself to censor the line of thought. Perhaps she was misinterpreting the Ambassador; to be fair, she remained silent and listened further.

"You haven't been back to Vulcan for some time," Soval continued. "You may find your assignment at the Ministry of Information refreshing."

T'Pol had serious doubts about that. Serving at the Ministry was tantamount to a demotion. She'd be greeting tourists, giving out directions and maps, suggesting sites of interest to visitors. It would scarcely be challenging.

It seemed ridiculous to waste her time performing

---

such trivial duties, when she was so critically needed aboard *Enterprise*.

Still, she did not bring up that subject quite yet; she knew Soval too well. Instead, she pursued a different issue. "I don't understand why I can't remain in San Francisco."

They moved away from the sidewalk, into a landscaped park.

"You've spent far too much time with humans," Soval answered swiftly. "It would be best if you return home for a while."

T'Pol now knew her suspicion had been correct. After spending time with the ship's crew, T'Pol had begun to formulate a hypothesis: Much of what Vulcans thought about humans was based on ignorance and prejudice. Vulcans remembered the extreme violence of their own past, and assumed humans were exactly the same, in need of the major transformation brought about by Surak, the pursuit of total nonemotion.

True, humans were still quite capable of violence, but they were far from the savagery that had marked ancient Vulcan history. In fact, humans were capable of much that was good, and they were remarkably adaptable, learning quickly from their mistakes. Their culture was making remarkable strides toward peace. T'Pol had learned they were loyal, well-meaning, and deserving of trust—something Soval would never give them.

Normally, she would have accepted Soval's pronouncement without question; now—having been "tainted" by her time amongst humans—she pressed. "You thought it was crucial to place a Vulcan on *Enterprise* during its first mission. . . . Why not now?"

Soval scrutinized her carefully. "You were there to provide logic to a crew of humans who insisted on leaving before they were ready." He paused. "But logic can't help them inside the Delphic Expanse."

T'Pol lifted her chin, mildly defiant. "Can you be certain of that?"

It was an impudent question; Soval did not answer it. Instead, his tone grew firm. "The High Command was quite specific. You're to return to Vulcan."

"I believe that should be *my* decision," T'Pol countered, her tone just as steely. There was strong inflection in her voice; she heard it, and realized that to a Vulcan who spent no time around humans, it would have sounded like an emotional outburst.

Soval stopped moving and turned to face her, his manner colder than the night air. "This is not a matter of choice. Defying the High Command would mean immediate dismissal. You know that."

T'Pol realized there was no point in bringing up her wish to remain on *Enterprise;* Soval had already made his position clear. He had anticipated her request, and was now supplying her with the answer: If she remained loyal to Captain Archer, she would do so at the cost of her diplomatic career.

Chapter 7

Archer was moving alongside Admiral Forrest, headed through the narrow corridors of the *Enterprise*. They were discussing T'Pol—in order to avoid discussing the fact that the two of them would probably never see each other again.

"I'm not surprised . . ." Forrest was saying. Archer had just informed him of the fact that the High Command had insisted on T'Pol's return to her homeworld.

"Soval agreed to let us take her back to Vulcan," the Captain said, "if it's all right with you." He was both glad and happy that Soval had said yes; it allowed everyone to spend more time with her—but perhaps saying good-bye now, quickly, would be easier.

Forrest of course nodded. He was not that far removed from the captaincy himself; he understood how attached crew members could become to each other—even if one of them was a Vulcan. "It's not that far out of your way."

He paused, keeping his tone brisk, businesslike. "How's the last refit team doing?"

"They're scheduled to be done by oh-six-hundred." Archer fell silent as the two of them reached an airlock.

On the other side was spacedock, and Earth. Archer could only hope it would be there when—if—he returned.

Forrest's expression softened. "I could tell you there're a lot of people counting on you . . . but I don't need to do that, do I?" The gratitude and pride in his quiet tone was unmistakable; Archer straightened, feeling a surge of respect for the man. It was no longer possible to ignore the fact that they most likely would never see each other again.

"No, sir."

The Admiral smiled faintly and extended his hand. "Good luck, Jon."

Not wanting to be maudlin, Archer did not respond; instead, he took the proffered hand. Forrest's grip was firm, reassuring. Archer returned it briefly, then watched as the Admiral made his way into the airlock.

Aboard the Klingon bird-of-prey, Duras was pacing the bridge. Patience; patience was what he needed most now, especially now that the time for battle had drawn near.

He had been forced to wait an agonizing span of days, far beyond the area of space surrounding Earth; *Enterprise*, Archer's ship, had been docked there, possibly for repairs, according to Duras's spies. There had been an attack on Archer's homeworld by an unknown foe—a fact that made Duras rejoice.

But it also made him grind his teeth during long nights without sleep. It would be suicide—suicide without honor—to try to locate Archer on Earth and kill him there. While Duras did not fear death, he feared failure; he dared not die until he fulfilled the chancellor's command, and brought Archer to justice.

So he had been forced to wait.

Now, word had come that, at long last, the *Enterprise* had pulled away from her moorings, and at last headed back into space.

Duras's pulse thrummed in his ears, a war cry. "Have they gone to warp?"

"Not yet," his first officer reported. He, too, sounded overeager; the days of boredom had worn on them all.

Duras issued an order, even though he knew his tactical officer would already be fulfilling it. "Charge weapons and prepare to bring them online!"

He sat, gaze wide, focused intently on the starlit viewscreen before him.

It was late, and the dimly lit *Enterprise* mess hall was empty, save for three denizens: Archer, Trip Tucker, and a half-empty bottle of Scotch. The Scotch, of course, belonged to Archer; he'd taken advantage of his time in San Francisco to pick up a few delicacies to brighten the long journey. He'd arrived first and procured a glass; Trip had followed soon after.

The Captain couldn't help wondering just how many others aboard the ship were finding it difficult to sleep. He was grateful that so far, only Trip had found his way to the mess hall. With Trip, at least, Archer could relax and let down his hair.

Unlike most days, the Captain sàt with his back to the windows. They were going to be at warp for a long, long time; he'd have his chance to get his fill of streaming warp stars.

He freshened his glass and peered over at Trip, whose dark blond hair was disheveled, no doubt the result of too much tossing and turning. "It's bad enough that *one* of us is up in the middle of the night," Archer groaned. He didn't mention, of course, that Trip had more reason than any of them to be up: losing someone you loved was tough enough, but to lose someone in such a catastrophic event, one that was constantly referred to, constantly in the news . . . How could Trip ever take his mind off it? Their mission was the direct result of the attack.

Even so, Archer did his best to treat Trip no differently than ever. It was what Archer had appreciated most when his dad had died: those people who acknowledged the fact, but treated him normally, the same as they always had.

"How's Porthos holding up?" Trip asked easily, his tone languid, faintly humorous—more like the old Trip than it had been in a long time. "If no *people* have returned from the Delphic Expanse, I doubt any *dogs* have."

Archer almost grinned at the image of a brave, all-canine crew . . . "He must be doing better than we are . . . He's fast asleep."

Each took a sip of his respective glass of Scotch.

Finally, Trip said, "Have you picked a new science officer?"

"No." Maybe he was in denial, but Archer had told himself that his subconscious could work on the choice, that he had too many things on his mind at present to contemplate a replacement. When the time came, he would know who to promote from within the crew.

Trip nodded. "You're gonna miss her, aren't you?"

Archer sighed; a corner of his lip twisted wryly. "When they first assigned her, I felt like strangling Soval . . ."

"She *does* kinda grow on you," Trip said.

Archer glanced up at him sharply, though not without humor. "I would think *you'd* be the first one to show her to the airlock."

Trip shrugged, cavalier. Another long, exhausted silence ensued, and then the engineer raised his glass. "To Henry Archer."

Archer lifted his eyebrows, puzzled.

By way of explanation, Trip said, "I wonder what he would've thought if he knew his engine was gonna help save the human race."

Archer, frankly, was glad his father *wasn't* there to see the attack, to feel the panic that afflicted everyone on Earth. His dad would have let him go into the Expanse, of course—but he would have been worried right into a coronary.

Archer swallowed a stiff belt of Scotch. It was single-malt, complexly fragrant, so smooth that he didn't even feel the urge to cough, though his eyes watered slightly at the alcoholic fumes.

"When I first got this job," he admitted softly, "commanding the first warp five ship was about as big a responsibility as I could've imagined. Then we began running into so many bad guys, I had to start thinking more about the safety of eighty-three people."

Trip leaned forward on his elbows, drink cupped in one hand, and gave a faint nod. "And now the stakes have gotten a lot bigger. . . ."

Archer looked down at his glass, and the amber liquid, reflecting starlight. "Weight of the world, Trip."

"Literally."

Trip belted back the remaining contents of his glass and refilled it; as he held the bottle, his gaze hardened.

"I can't wait to get in there, Captain . . . Find the people who did this." He set the bottle down and sought Archer's gaze. "Tell me we won't be tiptoeing around . . . None of that 'noninterference' crap T'Pol's always shoving down our throats . . ." He paused to take another swallow, then said, in a burst of anger that startled Archer, "Maybe it's a good thing she's leaving!"

There it was: grief masked as anger, a feeling the Captain had known all too well himself. His tone was soothing. "We'll do what we have to, Trip . . . whatever it takes."

Tucker seemed only mildly mollified; he fell sullenly silent.

Archer raised his glass—then nearly dropped it as the deck rocked abruptly, to the sound of a simultaneous *boom*. He and Trip stood—and almost fell back into their seats as the ship was hit again.

Duras, Archer thought, and managed to scramble for the door, without looking to see whether Trip was able to follow.

The bridge was rattling continually by the time Archer arrived; T'Pol, Reed, Hoshi, and Mayweather had all reported to their stations.

T'Pol looked up from her monitor the instant the Captain stepped foot on the bridge. "It's Duras," she reported.

Another *boom* echoed in Archer's ears, punctuating her words. He kept his balance as the deck lurched, and swiftly turned to Reed. "You've been wanting to test those new torpedoes. . . ."

Reed was clearly eager. "What yield, sir?"

"Start low. We just want to get them off our backs."

Reed responded at once, working the controls on his console.

Archer kept his gaze focused on the viewscreen, and watched as two bright flares streaked away from *Enterprise*, toward the bird-of-prey.

Duras swore beneath his breath as the ship around him vibrated fiercely, the result of two near-simultaneous, powerful blasts. As soon as he could be heard, he roared, "What was that?"

"Antimatter warheads," his tactical officer called, in a voice tinged with wonder.

Duras felt his own face contort with fury: his spies had said *Enterprise* was merely undergoing repairs—incompetent fools! All this time, the humans had been upgrading their weaponry, making Duras's task all the harder.

But he would not be outdone; too much was at stake. "Increase shielding and target their weapon ports!" he commanded.

It was *Enterprise*'s turn to do some vibrating of her own.

As the bird-of-prey returned fire, Archer struggled not to lose his balance and drop to the deck; as for Reed, he was clutching his console, teeth chattering as he yelled, "They're still on our backs, sir!"

"Bring the yield up," Archer commanded. No point in being gracious or wasting time; *Enterprise* didn't need to go into the Expanse already crippled. "Fifty percent."

Reed grinned faintly as he set to work.

Duras's head snapped back once, twice, in rapid succession, as though he had taken a personal blow.

His ship fared worse. He could feel the entire vessel heave upward and back along with him: he was momentarily dazzled as a section of circuit-lined bulkhead exploded onto the bridge in a brilliant fiery display. Debris whizzed a mere finger's breadth from his face.

For an instant, centripetal force held him captive in

his chair; the instant he could rise, he lurched toward his tactical officer and vented his rage. "I told you to target their weapon ports!"

The crewman shot him an unhappy but uncowed look; clearly, he had followed Duras's orders. "Their hull plating's been enhanced!"

Duras swore silently. If he survived his mission, he would surely see to it that his incompetent spies met their deaths.

Another blast threw him backwards against his chair.

His first officer turned to him, his expression one of desperation. "Our warp drive is failing!"

Duras ground his teeth so fiercely, flecks of enamel grazed his tongue. His every encounter with Archer seemed cursed, marked by failure and frustration. Were he superstitious, he would think Archer a demon, sent by Duras's ancestors as punishment for some crime the Klingon had inadvertently committed.

Once again, he was forced to call off the chase: *But only for a little while,* he promised himself. Only for a little while, and when the time was right, he would take the most savage possible revenge.

On *Enterprise,* Archer's adrenaline level was finally beginning to lower at the realization that the constant barrage had stopped, and the Klingon ship was slowing.

"They're dropping to impulse," Mayweather reported.

Archer turned to T'Pol. "How long will it take them to repair their engines?"

She looked up at him. "Impossible to determine . . ."

"Give me an educated guess," Archer said sharply. He was in no mood for Vulcan literalness at the moment.

She hesitated, clearly reluctant to rely on what she considered insufficient data. "Three hours . . . possibly more."

The Captain glanced back at Mayweather. "What's our speed?"

"Warp three, sir."

"Go to four-five," Archer ordered, then once again addressed T'Pol. "If we can make it to Vulcan space before they get their engines back . . . they'll think twice about giving us any trouble."

He took his chair, both determined . . . and deeply relieved that the battle was, for the time being, over.

At the same time, he definitely was *not* looking forward to arriving at Vulcan.

Archer was in the ready room, gazing pensively out at the streaming stars, when the door chimed.

"Come in."

T'Pol entered. She was not an easy read: most humans would never have noticed anything different about her behavior, but after spending a good deal of time with her in close quarters, Archer had begun to pick up on the subtler nuances of her manner. Right now, her tone and expression were subdued. She wanted to discuss a serious subject, and was not altogether comfortable doing so.

Oddly, Archer realized he was completely comfortable

in her presence. It certainly hadn't started out that way: she'd been an interloper, a spy for the Vulcans, cool and full of veiled verbal barbs at human frailty.

It hadn't helped either, that she'd been strikingly, exotically beautiful. Normally, Archer wouldn't have given her a second glance—he was accustomed to working with females, beautiful or not, and had no problem maintaining a professional attitude. So he didn't understand why he noticed T'Pol's attractiveness, and was uncomfortable around it; he decided, finally, that it was the fact that, unlike human women, she was utterly unaware of her beauty. It must have been the innocence; and in time, the effect wore off (or at least, the Captain convinced himself that it did).

Archer had gotten used to her, at the same time that she had gotten used to him and the rest of the crew. Either her attitude had done a one-eighty, or his had—but the fact was, despite the cultural differences, they had each come to respect each other.

"Ensign Mayweather says we're two days from Vulcan," she began.

She was unhappy about leaving *Enterprise*, Archer assumed; or maybe he was simply projecting his own feelings onto her. He wanted to do what he could to make things easier for her. He smiled warmly, and gestured. "Why don't you sit down?"

She sat, lean, long hands on her knees, her spine as always ramrod-straight, on the couch; Archer sat across from her.

"Just think," he said, meaning to cheer her up. "In two days, you'll be eating real Vulcan food."

The statement failed to have the effect he desired; she glanced down and away, an indication that his words only made what she had come to say more difficult. "Chef has done an adequate job of approximating Vulcan cuisine," she replied noncommitally.

"Well," Archer said with a heartiness he did not feel, "you never did care for the way we smell. . . . At least you won't have to put up with that anymore."

She looked up at him at last. "I've gotten used to it."

"How about all those emotions we bombard you with every day?" Archer was reaching desperately for something positive about T'Pol's departure, but she didn't seem to want to cooperate.

"I've grown accustomed to that as well . . ." She paused, then qualified her claim. "Somewhat."

"You're not making this easy," Archer said frankly. "There's gotta be something you're looking forward to back home."

She blinked, and parted her lips before blinking—for T'Pol, Archer had come to realize, the subtle gesture was equivalent to an emotional outburst in a human. "I don't wish to return to Vulcan," she said. "I want to remain on *Enterprise* . . . if you'll allow me to."

He stared at her; he would have been no more startled if she had collapsed in giggles. Vulcans did what Vulcans were told to do, and that was that. Vulcans never questioned authority; tradition and obedience were, to them, everything. "It's not a question of *my* allowing you," he said, when he found his voice. "The High Command would never agree to it."

"I've decided to resign my commission," she said.

His jaw dropped at that particular bombshell. T'Pol's parents and grandparents and great-grandparents, *ad infinitum,* had all been diplomats; for her to give up her career would be an unthinkable act of rebellion. And she had dedicated years of her life to that pursuit; was she truly willing now, to throw it all away?

"Why?" he asked, so stunned his voice dropped almost to a whisper. He recovered himself, then added, "You've worked so hard, T'Pol . . ."

Her tone was even and resolute; she had thought this through very carefully. "You're taking *Enterprise* into a very dangerous place. This is no time for me to leave."

Archer was touched beyond words. She was giving up something of supreme importance to her, even risking being disowned by family and friends, out of pure loyalty to him . . . and to the crew. "We'll be all right," he said warmly.

But she was past the point of being dissuaded. "You'll need a science officer . . . whether she's a member of the High Command or not."

"I've been thinking about who to promote . . ." Archer tried to counter, but she stopped him in a manner that either human or Vulcan could only describe as *impassioned.*

"You need *me,* Captain."

He couldn't contradict that. He could only stare at her a long while, with utter gratitude—and then he exited to the bridge before he was reduced to an emotional display that would only have embarrassed them both.

T'Pol followed him out.

Archer stepped up behind Mayweather, who was minding the helm.

"Keeping away from those Klingons isn't going to be as easy as we thought," the Captain said.

Mayweather swiveled his head to glance over his shoulder. "Sir?"

"We're not going to Vulcan," Archer announced, in a voice loud enough to be heard by the rest of the bridge crew. "Set a course for the Delphic Expanse."

In the periphery of his vision, he could see both Reed and Hoshi react with surprise to the news—but he paid them no heed. His gaze met T'Pol's, and for the first time, he saw a very recognizable, very human emotion reflected in her eyes: gratitude.

Chapter 8

**Captain's Starlog, supplemental. We've been travel-
ing at warp five for seven weeks . . . The crew is anxious to begin our mission.**

Along with the rest of his crew, Archer stared at the
bridge viewscreen. The edge of the infamous Delphic Expanse was now visible, as an incalculably vast column of
roiling, umber-colored clouds.

*It'll be like sailing into the middle of a Category-Five
hurricane,* Archer realized. How could anything with-
stand that kind of turbulence?

He forced himself to cancel the thought; he'd been
warned. He had never expected it to be easy—only
necessary.

"Distance?" he asked Mayweather.

"Nearly a million kilometers," the helmsman replied.

Trip let go a whistle of awe. "Looks a helluva lot closer than that . . ."

T'Pol looked up from her viewer, where she had been studying the phenomenon. "A common mistake when viewing an object of this size."

Archer tried to grasp the immensity of what he saw, and failed completely. He turned to Hoshi, at the communications console. "Magnify."

She obeyed; the image on the viewscreen faded into a new one: even more massive murky gray-brown clouds, swirling and colliding with each other in a disturbing, impressive display of turbulence. It remained impossible to see what lay beyond.

"Not very helpful," Trip commented dryly.

Mayweather's tone held a note of concern—with good cause, since he was the one who would have to navigate his way through this mess. "It's not that dense all the way through, is it?"

"The Vulcans said the Expanse is surrounded by thick layers of thermobaric clouds," Archer replied, with a calm he did not feel. "When their last ship went in, it took them almost six hours to get through it."

Mayweather nodded, his expression doubtful.

The Captain addressed T'Pol. "Anything on long-range scanners?"

"Nothing beyond the perimeter."

Archer eyed the viewscreen a long moment. There was no way to know what lay beyond, nothing to do save draw in a deep breath and trust Silik's time-traveling master, who had already proven himself capable of deceit. Yet Archer's instincts told him he had no other choice. "Point-two impulse, Travis. Let's head in."

Hours passed. Once it was clear that *Enterprise* could hold her own inside the treacherous-looking clouds, Archer retreated to his ready room and busied himself with the more mundane tasks required of the captaincy. He was impressed at how solid and steady the ship seemed, despite the apparent turbulence outside her.

Problem was, there weren't enough things to occupy his attention. Systems were operating smoothly; Travis had nothing new to report. After a long personal log entry, Archer found himself restless, a victim of what his dad used to refer to as the "hurry up and wait" syndrome.

He finally checked his chronometer: Time to be past the clouds, but a glance at the window revealed nothing but claustrophia-inducing, muddy opacity.

Archer rose and stepped out onto the bridge, where T'Pol was bent with elegant, infinite stoicism over her viewer.

"Anything?" the Captain asked her.

She turned toward him slightly, just enough to reveal the high angle of her cheekbone. "Not yet."

Hoshi spoke, her tone faintly irritable, anxious. "We've been in here more than six hours."

"Let's be patient," Archer said. It occurred to him that

perhaps the Vulcans were capable of greater warp speed than they were letting on, which is why the *Vaankara* had made it through in six hours. It might take *Enterprise* longer; at any rate, there was no point in getting rattled about it. He suspected they'd have enough things to worry about once they made it into the Expanse itself.

He glanced up as Trip entered the bridge from the turbolift.

"We launched the communications buoy, sir," the engineer reported, his manner one of businesslike satisfaction. Trip's dark mood seemed to have lifted, now that they were finally getting somewhere. "We got a test signal through to Starfleet."

Archer nodded, pleased, and addressed Hoshi. "Keep them apprised of our position."

"Aye, sir." She seemed grateful to have something to do.

T'Pol's console beeped; she frowned slightly into her viewer. Archer stepped up and stood shoulder-to-shoulder with her, concerned.

"Got something?" he asked. He had not forgotten the fact that Duras was probably still in pursuit.

"Yes." She remained bent over her scanner, clearly trying to determine precisely what it was she was looking at.

"Probably the buoy," Trip offered.

"Not unless you launched three of them," T'Pol replied. She straightened and gave Archer a sharp look.

Even before it came, the captain tensed for the first blast; when it arrived, the deck rocked beneath his feet.

He stumbled forward, caught hold of the nearest console, while beside him, T'Pol held fast to her viewer.

The instant he regained his balance, he scrambled to his chair over the sound of the Tactical Alert klaxon.

On the viewscreen, three Klingon birds-of-prey sailed out of the thermobaric clouds; Archer watched as their dazzling weapons fire illuminated the murkiness with an eerie glow.

Aboard the Klingon vessel, Duras watched as two of three disruptor blasts missed the *Enterprise*.

Patience, he told himself, *patience . . .*

But the word had a hollow ring. Duras was past waiting, past caring whether he followed the chancellor's orders. He wanted only one thing: the taste of Archer's blood in his mouth, *now.*

A peculiar madness had overtaken him: he had given up eating, sleeping, given up all pursuits except the thought of Archer. He'd heard of warriors developing such obsessions; there were tales in his culture's oral history of the misfortunes that had befallen soldiers whose lust for the kill burned too hotly, leading to carelessness. But Duras could no longer help himself. The human haunted his waking dreams; there were times, on the bridge—for Duras would no longer leave it, even to rest the prescribed number of hours—when he thought he sensed Archer standing just behind him, felt the warmth of the human's breath upon his neck.

He would propel himself from his chair and whirl

about, ready to strike, to let loose a crippling blow, a battle cry . . . only to see empty air. Then he would feel his crewmen's gaze upon him, and turn back to see them eyeing him with candid expressions of doubt.

They were eyeing him now, as he rose from his chair to stand no more than an arm's breadth from the screen, wishing he could reach through the vacuum of space with his bare fist and seize the *Enterprise*, crush it to powder.

He *was* mad, Duras knew; Archer possessed his mind and soul like an ancestral ghost. But he did not care.

At the realization that two-thirds of the disruptor fire had missed its target, he gave his tactical officer a wildly vicious glance.

The stare prompted an immediate explanation from the frustrated crewman. "The targeting scanners won't lock on!"

"Then get closer," Duras said so that his first officer would hear and comply.

If he had to ram the Earth ship from the sky using his own vessel, he would. He had come too far, and nothing would stop him now. . . .

Enterprise shook continuously as the Klingon vessels coordinated their attack. Archer did his best to hang on. Three against one: it wasn't looking good, even with fancy torpedoes and new hull plating, but the Captain wasn't about to give up.

If the time traveler had been telling the truth, then *En-*

terprise had a good chance of making it safely into the Expanse—which meant that there had to be a way to lose the Klingons.

Archer just had to think of one.

Besides, he'd be damned before he'd let Duras win.

His voice vibrating, Trip yelled, "I thought you said Klingons wouldn't go into the Expanse!"

"We're not in the Expanse yet!" Archer yelled back. He leaned forward and called to Mayweather, "Hold your course, go to full impulse!"

Trip's voice was filled with concern for his engines. "I wouldn't recommend that, Captain! The intake manifolds are having a tough enough time as it is!"

Archer registered the complaint and mentally filed it away, but did not reply. The condition of the intake manifolds were not a top priority: remaining alive was. His tone steady, he told the helmsman, "You heard me, Travis."

A tense silence ensued—interminably long seconds passed, and then Mayweather reported, "They're keeping up with us, sir."

A fresh blast *boomed* in Archer's ears; his brain scarcely had the chance to interpret the signal before a second blast followed.

"We're being hailed," Hoshi called.

"Put it up," Archer said.

After a heartbeat, an image coalesced on the viewscreen: that of Duras, looking unkempt and haggard, eyes wild, his face looming so large that Archer could see chips and cracks on the points of his sharpened teeth.

"Surrender," Duras said, in a voice that combined a hiss with a growl, "or be destroyed!"

Archer looked at him with unalloyed hatred; he thought of Kolos, the wise old advocate who had defended him from Duras's lies—and for his efforts, was sent to the hostile environs of the Rura Penthe penal colony. Because of Duras, Kolos—one of the most honorable men Archer had ever known, Klingon or not—might well be dead. At best, he was suffering incredible torment each waking hour.

"Go to Hell," he told Duras, with deep satisfaction; he'd been longing to express the sentiment to his pursuer's face for some time.

The Klingon literally snarled. "You're outgunned, Archer. Come about and prepare to be boarded. If you don't obey my orders, I'll—"

Archer made a chopping motion with his hand; Hoshi immediately pressed a control, and the viewscreen darkened, then changed to the image of the deadly birds-of-prey nestled in the clouds. The Captain was in no mood to listen to Duras's threats; he had a ship to save . . . otherwise, Earth was doomed.

"The perimeter clouds are dissipating." T'Pol pressed a series of controls at her console, then brought her gaze back to her viewer. "I'm detecting clear space ahead . . ."

"That's why Duras wants us to come about," Archer murmured to himself. "He's afraid of the Expanse." More loudly, he told Mayweather, "Increase speed, Travis."

* * *

Aboard the bird-of-prey, the Klingon first officer turned to face his commander; on his face was a look of concern—not so much for the situation, but for the effect his words would have on Duras. "The other ships are signaling. . . . They're going to turn back."

It was clear from his tone that the first officer was suggesting *they* turn back, too—a notion that so enraged Duras, he would have struck the officer dead, had he not been working with a skeleton crew.

"Cowards!" he screamed at the viewscreen, where the image of the other two Klingon ships hovered. Spittle flew from his lips. He no longer cared whether his ship survived to report Archer's death; Duras was prepared to fight to the death, even though he had strict orders to bring himself and his prisoner back to the Klingon homeworld alive.

He became aware once again of his two crewman staring at him; clearly, they awaited an order to follow the other ships, to break off and return home.

Home, to defeat and utter shame, not just upon him, but upon his entire House.

Duras looked on them both with contempt. "We'll do it ourselves," he muttered darkly.

The tactical officer blinked in disbelief, his face a mask of cowardice. "We're too close to the Expanse . . ."

Before he could utter another word, Duras bolted to his feet and threw the crewman from his chair. He took the helm himself, hatred burning in him like an unquenchable flame.

*   *   *

Archer watched as the bridge viewscreen revealed one of the birds-of-prey veering away from the others, back into the thick column of thermobaric clouds. A second ship soon followed. . . .

The Captain held his breath, waiting. But the third ship—he knew instinctively it had to be Duras's—held its course.

"Only one left, sir," Reed reported from tactical, the same relief Archer felt in his tone.

He scarcely uttered the words when the bridge shuddered violently again beneath a volley of blasts from the remaining vessel.

"Keep firing," he ordered Reed.

T'Pol reported from her station, her tone curt, clipped. "The Expanse is less than five minutes away."

"Maybe he'll turn around, like his friends," Trip volunteered hopefully.

Archer's tone was grim; he knew Duras too well. "I wouldn't bet on it."

A fresh series of booms echoed in Archer's ears; the *Enterprise* reeled under the shock. Archer leaned forward and said swiftly to Reed, "Your new torpedoes aren't having the same effect as last time."

Reed's hands flew over his controls; he glanced down at a readout, then answered just as quickly, "Duras transferred his aft shields forward. Our weapons can't penetrate them."

The ship convulsed again—this time, harder than before. Archer instinctively sensed damage, even before

Trip turned to him from his station. The engineer's tone was high-pitched with tension. "We just lost three anti-matter injectors, Captain! Any more, and we're in big trouble!"

Archer understood Trip's concern—without the warp engines, their mission would fail before it had even begun—but could spare no time to acknowledge it; Reed's last statement had prompted an idea. Moving unsteadily because of the repeated jolts courtesy of Duras, the Captain stepped over to T'Pol.

"If he's transferred his shielding forward," Archer asked the Vulcan, "what's protecting his stern?"

Another ear-splitting explosion; Trip heard the Captain's question, and out of frustration shouted, "Does it matter? *He's* chasing *us!*"

Archer steadfastly ignored the engineer, and repeated, more intensely, to T'Pol, *"What's protecting his stern?"*

"Minimal shielding," she replied.

Archer forced himself to think, despite the constant barrage of deafening *booms*. At last, he turned to Mayweather.

"You think you can pull off an L-4 at this speed?"

It was a risky maneuver for a ship the *Enterprise's* size, even if she was trickling slower than syrup in winter. The Captain wasn't even sure that Mayweather would have heard of the "death-defying loop," as it was also called, as if it were a circus act.

It may as well have been: It was as dangerous as a high-wire act, without the net. But if Archer trusted anyone to pull it off, it was Travis Mayweather. And at this particular moment, he didn't have much choice: it was the L-4, or death at the hands of a crazed Klingon.

The helmsman's expression actually brightened at the challenge. "I can try, sir."

"Then look for the densest cloud formation you can find," Archer instructed. Too bad the idea hadn't come to him earlier; now, the clouds were beginning to peter out.

The Captain stepped over to a companel and activated the shipwide intercom. "Captain Archer to all hands . . ." He paused, searching for precisely the right words, and finally settled for a passionate "Hang on!"

He glanced up at the viewscreen. Although they were currently sailing through an area of thinner vapor, a thick, ominously dark cluster of clouds lay dead ahead.

"That one looks good to me," he told Mayweather, as he took his seat.

The helmsman seized the manual controls—the computer certainly wouldn't have permitted such a risky maneuver—and navigated *Enterprise* straight into the clouds.

Inside the ship there was only a minimal sense of disorientation; life support and gravity systems kept the ride tolerable, even as the Captain was pushed back in his chair by the g-forces. But Archer could tell from the viewscreen that his vessel was beginning to head upward in an arc more extreme than any amusement-park roller coaster.

* * *

At the helm of the bird-of-prey, Duras stared at the viewscreen through eyes wide with mania. He had thrown his tactical officer aside with such fury that the crewman had struck his head forcefully against a bulkhead, and now lay sprawled on the deck.

His first officer remained at his post—clearly reluctant to obey his wild-eyed commander, but at the same time, apparently unwilling to be killed for disobeying an order.

And Duras was well beyond the point of being willing to kill one of his own crewman for disobeying him.

Archer directed his ship into a dark thicket of clouds, perhaps thinking this would discourage pursuit; no matter. Duras followed. He would continue to follow into the Expanse, and beyond, if need be, despite the fact that the High Council forbade all Klingon ships from entering the area because of its infamous dangers.

Through the clouds the bird-of-prey sailed; *Enterprise* was lost visually, swallowed up by the murky opacity. No matter. Soon, the Klingon ship emerged in an area of clearer space.

Confident in his madness, Duras glanced back up at the viewscreen—and immediately did a double take. In the distance were more scattered columns of clouds . . . but no *Enterprise*.

"Where are they?" he demanded, aghast; his first officer did not reply, having lapsed into sullen silence some time earlier.

Impossible, Duras told himself. Insane or not, he still knew that ships did not simply disappear.

*　　*　　*

Archer clutched the arms of his command chair as Mayweather guided the *Enterprise* into a gigantic loop that, at one point, had her belly pointed in the direction the crew considered "up"; at that point, the ship was completely inverted, but Travis finished scribing the arc and brought her down so that she gracefully righted herself and came soaring out of the clouds—directly behind the bird-of-prey.

"Fire," Archer said.

Lips compressed, gaze intent on his controls, Malcolm Reed unleashed a barrage on the enemy ship.

Archer watched as the photonic torpedoes—appearing on the viewscreen as bright, round flares—streaked away from *Enterprise* toward the rear of the Klingon ship.

Duras had been so focused on firing the disruptors—his one thought that of blowing Archer and his crew to the afterlife—that he quite failed to notice the small, blinking display on his console, with its attendant bleating alarm, showing a bevy of bright red dots moving rapidly toward his unprotected stern.

Perhaps his first officer was about to yell out, to alert him; Duras got only the most fleeting impression of the crewman whirling toward him in that last, fleeting second.

And then the bridge on which he sat began to dissolve.

It was the roar he noticed first: the pounding of blood in his ears, the shriek of the ship, so loud he could hear nothing else, not even the sound of his own frustrated screaming. Then came crimson flecked with gold, brilliant, blinding, blotting out the sight of exploding consoles, shattering bulkheads. Duras drew a breath; fire filled his lungs, seared away his hair.

He tried to draw another, and realized there was no more air to be had: Life support systems had failed. Deafened, sightless, he flailed, and felt himself begin to lift out of his chair : Gravity was failing, too.

In his final, fiery millisecond before he was hurled into the vacuum of space, the Klingon allowed himself one last spasm of hatred for Archer, and wondered: Would he, Duras, be considered a failure in his mission? Would his House continue to feel shame on his behalf, or would his kin instead find honor in his death?

He had not given up, as the others had; he had not turned back. He had persevered, to the end. . . .

There was a sudden flare of brightness, of intense heat that took him to a place far beyond pain . . . and then it faded abruptly, leaving only infinite darkness.

Chapter 9

Archer watched the viewscreen as, in front of them, the bird-of-prey exploded in an angry red blaze that momentarily lit up the dark clouds like a fleeting sunset.

Enterprise sailed through the flames and debris smoothly, as if she were moving through clear space.

Archer let go a sigh. He took no joy in Duras's death—though he could not admit to sorrow, either. He had done everything he could to avoid violence, to discourage the Klingon from following—and, indeed, the saner ones on two of the birds-of-prey had wisely chosen to back off, and return home. Duras had been determined to make this a fight to the death; he simply hadn't realized that Archer was just as equally determined not to lose.

The Captain let go the grim thought and instead directed a faint grin at his helmsman; Archer had to admit to being impressed. "Nice going, Travis."

Mayweather half turned to him; for the first time, the

Captain noticed the beads of sweat on the young helmsman's dark forehead. "I hope you don't ask me to do that
too often, sir."

Archer's grin grew indulgent; it was interrupted by an
announcement from a relieved-sounding Hoshi Sato.

"The Expanse is ahead, Captain."

He gazed up at the viewscreen. In the far distance, the
clouds were thinning out, giving way to clear space. He
looked at it a long moment before finally asking Trip,
"Did you lose any more of those injectors?"

"No, sir," Tucker replied. His tone was calm—no doubt
in part because the battle was over, and his engines were
safe . . . but Archer also got the impression that Trip was
deeply relieved to have finally arrived at their destination, to have the mission truly underway.

The Captain turned to T'Pol, his expression a bit
whimsical. "Sure you still want to tag along?"

It was the one thing about her that had always impressed him, from the first time he'd met her: She was
the one Vulcan who understood a joke, and knew how to
play along.

"It's only logical," she answered.

Archer stared back at the viewscreen. After a long silence, he said, "Let's see what's in there."

Enterprise leapt toward the distant stars.

Her passage did not go unnoticed.

At the great round table in the inner sanctum, Degra
studied the blinking, brightly colored icon of the Earth

ship as it moved slowly through the cartographic representation of stars and planets, each labeled in one of the five major Xindi tongues. In deference to the aquatic members of the group, nothing but the dim glow from the graphics lit the room, leaving the others in shadow.

Degra was but one of ten Xindi at the table. Beside him sat his aide, Mallora; the two were flanked on one side by a pair of reptilians, on the other by a pair of slow-moving, heavily furred marsupials. Between the former and latter, two insectoids sat, and a pair of aquatics undulated in a water-filled tank.

Externally, Xindi politics were complicated, with myriad parties separated according to species; ethnic tension was the rule, with different groups occasionally forming alliances in order to seize control from the others. Theoretically, most of the governments on the divided homeworld were republics.

True rulership, however, had always belonged to the sanctum. It had been thus for millennia, long before the emergence of representative governments; Degra's position of power was a legacy from his ancestors. He had been groomed for it since childhood, as had all the others surrounding him.

And like the others, he had learned upon entering the sanctum to leave all racial tensions and preconceived ideas outside. Indeed, a sense of equality was encouraged here; for such reason, the table was round.

Things had certainly not been equal outside, in the Xindi world. From an evolutionary perspective, the aquatics had attained intelligence first—but not being land-based had led to theirs being a relatively peaceable society. They demanded a political voice only when the land-based races began to despoil their waters.

Degra's race, with its primate ancestry, had been next to attain a very high degree of intelligence; it troubled him, for a reason he could not fathom, to discover that, of all the Xindi species, his resembled the people of Earth most closely.

The primates had, for eons, ruled most of the Xindi world; they had been ruthless in their oppression of the other land species, and in their dogma that the other races were inferior. Although they had, over the past few centuries, abandoned that belief (ostensibly, at least), they were still hated by the others, most notably the reptilians and the insectoids.

To date, Degra's people still controlled most of the planet . . . but the reptilian warrior class was rapidly gaining power, and the quickly reproducing insectoids had become the most populous group. Originally, Degra and most primate politicians had thought these things a tragedy; certainly, they could only lead to more racial wars of the sort that had nearly torn the planet apart. The oft-stated belief shared by the primates was that the reptilians (their intelligence having evolved from only their brain stems and basal ganglia) thought with their spinal cords . . . and the insectoids, of course, didn't think at all. And the marsupials . . . well, the marsupials thought, all right; they thought about napping upside down in trees.

Now, with the threat of annihilation from Earth, Degra's perspective had changed. He was grateful to the warriors for their willingness to sacrifice themselves; their ferocity in combat could now be put to good use.

In a way, he was even grateful to the people of Earth, for giving the Xindi a new group to hate. It was a most unifying experience. For a time, only the ten members of the sanctum had been privy to the information concerning the future destruction of the planet—but they voted, after lengthy discussion, to inform the entire population. At once, petty wars and local rioting stopped; even the notoriously skeptical insectoids put their support behind the anti-Earth efforts, and presented lavish donations to the little reptilians orphaned by their warrior-father, who had manned the probe.

Today, however, the atmosphere in the sanctum was charged with conflict. Degra, made wise by his fifty journeys around his homeworld's sun, sat back in the shadows and listened. His aide, Mallora, whose hair had not yet begun to silver, was talking, shaking his head subtly as a token of his general disagreement with the others.

Mallora's tone was impassioned. "It could simply be a coincidence."

Beside him, Guruk looked down on him with condescension, narrowing opaque yellow eyes with vertical slits for pupils. Reptilians' expressions were unreadable, masklike—with all the animation of a lizard sunning itself upon a rock, Degra thought—but the contempt in Guruk's tone was unmistakable. "You're being naive.

Their planet is fifty light-years away. It's not a coincidence." Guruk was alarmingly tall, even for his race; his voice was low, emanating from deep within his chest, and his sibilants were marked by a slight hiss. He shifted his weight, causing the faint light to ripple across the scales covering his face and muscular arms; the effect was prismatic, throwing off glints of amber, ruby, emerald.

Of all the races, only the reptilian and the primate tended to intermix. Degra had always thought it was because of the striking beauty of the reptilian skin. He had been told it was softer than it appeared, though he had never himself touched it. The notion of embracing a creature with a darting forked tongue, scales, and vesti‑ gial tail disgusted him; and then there was the matter of a cloaca. Old prejudices died hard.

Mallora did not appreciate Guruk's tone or his words. He countered forcefully. "How do you know your contacts gave you accurate information? The ship may not be from Earth."

At that point, Shresht, the head insectoid at the table, let go a shrill blast caused by rubbing his darkly gossamer wings together. It was a request for attention; the others faced him at once. Like Degra, they did not possess the equipment to reproduce the insectoid language, but they understood it. Their mastery of the language was not out of deference to Shresht's race, but the fact that its members lacked the teeth, tongue, and palate necessary to articulate primate speech, which had, after centuries of primate domination, become the planet's official language.

Even the aquatics—by nature serene and emotionally removed from conflict—turned swiftly in unison inside their tank, their soft, translucent dorsal fins flowing delicately above them. Their names were Qam and Qoh; beneath their pale, moon-shaped and -colored faces, gills released bubbles that ascended slowly to the surface of their private sea. Degra had never been able to tell the two of them apart, nor was there a clear distinction as to which one held more power, or even as to whether they were male, female, or a mixed pair. Aquatic politics were based on equality and consensus, a concept foreign to the land-based species.

Judged by the standards of any other Xindi group, insectoid behavior seemed manic. Degra had endured a great deal of cultural training which enlightened him to the fact that, since insectoids were shorter-lived and lacked the protection of an internal skeleton, they had developed mannerisms based on a sense of urgency.

But the torrent of clicks and chirps Shresht unleashed on this particular day was more hysterical than usual.

It's the beginning of an invasion! Hundreds of other ships will follow them!

Degra translated the outburst silently in his head, and, once again, left Mallora to do the speaking for him.

"They have no way of knowing that *we* launched that probe."

Shresht only grew more agitated. *We must destroy the vessel!*

Guruk listened with great focus and stillness—a stillness, Degra knew, hid a reptilian penchant for sudden, deadly strikes. At last, the reptilian asked, "How many humans are aboard?"

Shresht's chirps grew so high-pitched Degra longed to cover his ears. *It doesn't matter! They've come to find the weapon! They must be destroyed!*

Beneath his glistening black carapace, his thorax began to pulse and twitch in agitation; he flailed his slender, fine-haired limbs. Beside him, his aide followed suit, in a display of insectoid outrage and fear.

Degra said nothing, and directed a look at Mallora to silence him. Arguing with Shresht was pointless; any attempts to reason with him now would be wasted.

Slowly, deliberately, an old marsupial covered in thick, graying fur turned toward Degra. This was the great, hulking Narsanyala. He formed his question with such languor that Degra fought to keep his patience. "When will it be ready?"

It was easy to believe, given the marsupials' tendency toward torpor, that they were harmless and stupid, but such was not the case. Narsanyala's people, while they much preferred the company of family, were shrewd when it came to politics, and had proven themselves fierce fighters when attacked. Degra looked down at Narsanyala's hands, and the fingers that terminated in thick, sharp black claws; while the marsupial was by nature affable, he was also capable of slitting Degra open from throat to pubis with a single strong swipe.

"The next series of tests are being prepared," Degra answered tersely. He wished to give no further information; the primates, possessed of the greatest engineering talent, had taken control of the weapons project. And with good reason: The reptilians and insectoids would rush headlong into attacking Earth well before the Xindi were ready—and the marsupials and aquatics would dally too long, and permit the homeworld to be destroyed.

As expected, Shresht reacted with another shrill outburst of insectoid.

You said your "test" was successful! You said the probe did what it was designed to do.

A muscle in Degra's lean, sculpted cheek twitched, but his tone remained even as he countered, "The new weapon is far more complex."

Facial skin flashing like dull jewels, Guruk turned to look down upon Degra. The cadence of the reptilian's speech was slower, calmer than that of the insectoid's, but it was clear he agreed with Shresht. "We'll accomplish nothing if all you do is run tests."

His aide hissed agreement; the insectoids let go a cacophony of whistles, chirps, chatters.

True to his character, Narsanyala raised his voice just loud enough to be heard above the din. "We must be patient . . . follow the plan we all agreed to."

He graced Degra with a glance indicating support; grateful, Degra returned it. There was a certain wisdom in the design of the Xindi world: The passion of the reptilians and insectoids was balanced out by the coolness of the marsupials and aquatics.

And, of course, Degra secretly believed the primates were meant to be leader of them all.

While he ostensibly agreed with Mallora that the appearance of the Earth ship *might* be coincidence, it was certainly an uncomfortable one, and one that needed to be further examined. For that, he would rely on the reptilians' military talents.

He turned to Guruk, and said softly, "Learn everything you can about this human vessel."

At once, the chattering of the insectoids eased; Guruk hissed his approval.

Degra let his gaze fall once again upon the computer readout in the table's center, and the bright, blinking representation of the human vessel.

Whatever the reason for its appearance, it would certainly have to be destroyed.

T'Pol sat in what had become *Enterprise*'s command center—a large, dark chamber filled with monitor stacked upon monitor, most of which were unused, the screens a dull opaque gray. A large, brightly lit display dominated the wall before her: a starchart of the Expanse. On one edge, a single planet circling a star blinked, indicating their current destination.

On this particular day, T'Pol wore civilian clothing, a low-cut V neck suit in a shade of bright steel blue with a white belt slung low on the hip, far too outspoken for a Vulcan diplomatic aide. Upon rising, she had stood before her tiny closet and reached, out of habit, for her usual drab Vulcan uniform—then dropped her hand.

One Earth month and eleven days had passed since they had entered the Expanse, and she had failed to realize, after all that time, that she no longer had the right to wear it. That troubled her—not that she had lost the right, but that she had not remembered.

So she forced herself to remember, in that instant, all she had surrendered: her future as a diplomat representing her planet, a goal she had clung to since childhood; the respect of her peers; and even the approval of her own family. She had not shamed them by attempting to contact them; they had certainly been notified by the Embassy, and chosen not to communicate with her. She could not question their choice. It was the right of families to disown offspring who broke with family tradition, and most of T'Pol's ancestors had been diplomats since the time of Surak. She had to assume that she was no longer on speaking terms with any of her kin.

She was also violating a Vulcan principle by going off with a shipload of humans, armed with weapons and—at least, from her culture's perspective—bent on destroying another world to protect their own. This went against T'Pol's own beliefs; but she possessed one thing her Vulcan contemporaries did not.

Trust in Captain Archer, and his crew. While her—*former*, T'Pol forced herself to add mentally—superior, Ambassador Soval, saw humans as completely incapable of

123

rational thought, T'Pol had been the first Vulcan to truly work among humans. True, they were highly emotional; but Archer and his officers tempered their emotion with compassion and logic. She trusted them to shun violence whenever possible, even in their attempt to stop the Xindi.

That morning, T'Pol had put a hand upon her Vulcan uniform and pulled it from the closet. It was illogical to keep it; she moved to pull it from the hanger, intending to throw it into the recycler . . . But something stayed her hand. It seemed more than a uniform; it was an entire life.

Tentatively, she put the uniform back in the closet.

And then she chose one of the brightest colors of the civilian clothes she'd brought, and slipped into the suit without pause. At the mirror, she carefully combed her hair into the style most approved by the diplomatic corps; only then did she hesitate, and stare at her image for a few seconds. The distraction of being in the Expanse, and giving up her career, had caused her to forego her usual trims; her bangs and the hair at the nape of her neck had grown longer. She most definitely no longer looked the part of a Vulcan ambassador's aide.

Quite deliberately, she put her fingers into her hair and tousled it. She was a renegade now, no longer bound by tradition. She was a civilian who had cast her lot with humans, and there was no point in maintaining an unnecessary degree of formality.

After breakfast, she'd reported to the command center for duty. To her surprise—she was always early, arriving before anyone else—Lieutenant Reed was already there, as well as Captain Archer. Reed noticed the difference in her appearance at once, and did a mild double take, which he immediately suppressed; Archer did not even notice.

The captain was seated at one of the monitors, his expression almost as grim as the day he had first announced the attack on Earth; his brow was deeply furrowed, making him look older than he was. The strain of the situation was wearing on him; a Vulcan commander would realize the logic of having to endanger those on his ship in order to achieve a greater good, but T'Pol imagined the situation was different for a human. Since she had first met Archer, she had noted his tendency to take the safety of every crew member personally, as if he were responsible for any harm that came to them.

"Good morning, Captain, Lieutenant," T'Pol said upon entering. Greetings were illogical and unnecessary, but, as a diplomat, T'Pol had been trained in such idle pleasantries.

"Morning, Sub-Commander," Reed answered.

Archer did not reply, did not even glance up.

T'Pol took her place and set to work.

Time passed before the captain finally spoke; he did not meet her gaze. His tone was uncharacteristically tense. "How long till we get there?"

T'Pol did not need to check the chronometer; she had noticed the time upon her arrival, and made the calculation easily in her head. She also knew, because of her time on Earth, not to answer accurately, *another two hours, fifty-one minutes, twenty-four seconds*, which humans would find annoying. She rounded the figure up. "Another three hours."

Lieutenant Reed swiveled in his chair to face Archer. "Did the freighter captain say who we're supposed to contact?"

The Captain kept his gaze focused on his monitor screen. "The foreman of the north mine . . . he's expecting us."

T'Pol took the opportunity to ask a question, one that Archer had not answered. Of late, he had been reticent concerning details. "What makes this captain so certain one of the miners is Xindi?"

Archer sighed and at last looked up from the screen. "He's not. He just said he 'thinks' there was a Xindi aboard a transport he took there a few years ago."

"And it's safe to enter orbit?" Reed's voice was plainly skeptical. "There are no security considerations?" Security was the Lieutenant's responsibility, a task he took most seriously; apparently, the Captain and Commander Tucker seemed to think he sometimes took it *too* seriously, and often joked about the fact.

But Archer's reply was anything but good-humored; T'Pol heard the undercurrent of anger in his tone. "He didn't mention any."

Reed's expression grew troubled. "With all due respect, sir, we should approach with caution. The freighter captain was of questionable character."

T'Pol watched as forty-one days of frustration rose in Archer and consumed the last of his patience. The Captain swiveled to face Reed, and addressed him like an angry teacher confronting a particularly dull schoolboy. "Where are we, Malcolm?"

Reed colored slightly. "Sir?"

"This room," Archer demanded, jerking his head at the surroundings while keeping his gaze fastened on the Lieutenant, "what did it used to be?"

Reed hesitated, clearly at a loss to understand Archer's questions or the sudden heat in his tone. "It was a storage bay, sir . . . conduit housings, I believe."

"But it got retrofitted," Archer stated flatly. "Starfleet went to a lot of trouble to turn it into our new command center. Why's that, Malcolm?"

T'Pol thought she understood where the Captain's hostile interview was leading, but Lieutenant Reed was still hopelessly confused. "Because of our . . . mission, sir."

"To find the Xindi, right?"

"Right," Reed echoed, uncertain.

Archer leaned forward for emphasis. "So this state-of-the-art equipment was put in here to help us gather all the pieces of the puzzle . . . figure out who's trying to destroy Earth . . ."

"Right," Reed said, but his expression clearly asked, *Where's he going with this?*

Archer made a sweeping gesture at the cutting-edge technology surrounding them; at last, he gave his frustration full rein and let his voice rise in anger. "Six weeks!"

he exclaimed. "We've been in this Expanse for six weeks. What data have we gathered? What pieces of the puzzle have we started to put together? Not a single one! Humanity's in trouble, Malcolm. We don't have the luxury of being safe or cautious. And if the only lead we can find comes from a 'freighter captain of questionable character,' then that's good enough for me. Understood?"

Reed straightened and projected the essence of pure military formality and respect. "Understood."

His answer did nothing to mollify the Captain's helpless ire. Archer rose, expression still taut, and left the chamber without a word.

Reed shared a look with T'Pol; his expression clearly asked, *Is it me, or has the Captain finally gone mad from the responsibility?*

It was a good question. T'Pol had come this far because she had trusted Archer not to react rashly to the threat, but to deal with it fairly, logically. It had never occurred to her that Archer might actually break under the strain.

She said nothing to Reed, merely fixed her gaze firmly back on her monitor and returned to her work.

Chapter 10

In the *Enterprise* mess, Hoshi Sato picked up her tray of tofu Thai curry and gazed out at the crowded room. There was little room left at the tables—which had been her intention. Normally, she took lunch at a later hour, in order to avoid the rush, but she had noticed every day when she arrived that the MACOs—the soldiers belonging to the Military Assault Command Operations—were just leaving.

For the past month and a half, Hoshi had had little to do. She'd managed to finish reading *Languages of the Sub-Sahara* after all; for some reason, she'd assumed she'd be too busy to get through it. So far, the Expanse hadn't been dangerous at all . . . only boring.

It wouldn't last, she knew . . . but at the moment, there was nothing for a linguist–cum–communications officer to do, no alien languages to translate, no incoming messages—only a great deal of tension on the bridge while everyone waited.

In the meantime, Hoshi wanted to be helpful. One thing she'd noticed was that the soldiers assigned to help with the mission weren't mixing at all with the crew; after all this time, she didn't even know their names, and she figured it might be a good thing to make friends with them. Perhaps she could serve as an unofficial liaison of sorts.

And so she pretended to scan carefully for vacant seats, then to notice that there just happened to be room at the table where the MACOs were sitting.

MACOs. At first she'd mispronounced it "May-co," and when Malcolm Reed had corrected her, saying, "That's 'Mah-co,'" she'd retorted, with linguistlike speed:

"What are they, sharks?"

She hadn't understood then why the normally repressed Reed had burst out laughing—not until she had seen her first soldier, and noticed the insignia on the breast of his gray camouflage jumpsuit: an inverted delta of a blue shark, teeth bared, aswim in a dark sea. The MACO probably had no idea why Hoshi smiled at him so broadly as he passed.

Since then, she had learned all she could about the organization—there'd been little else to do, anyway. She had known little about the military then, but she knew now that the MACOs were regarded as the most elite of all the organizations. Ninety-five percent of all cadets dropped out of the program within the first three months, and those who remained would be further tested until a mere one percent made it, three hard years later, to graduation. Their motto: *Ever Invincible.* A MACO never surrendered . . : and did whatever was necessary to win. She'd noticed wryly during her search for information that getting a MACO mad at you was considered tantamount to suicide.

At the same time, the organization's members were legendary for their courtesy and strict code of honor. That fact had crept into Earth languages, too, producing the expression, "I'd sooner trust a MACO than my own mother."

Now, Hoshi smiled at the four soldiers who sat, off to themselves, at a table in the corner of the mess hall, and moved over to the table.

"Is this seat taken?" she asked warmly. Being a linguist had its advantages when it came to dealing with people. Being fascinated by others' speech meant that she found them fascinating, as well; she'd always been outgoing—another good reason for her to serve as liaison. If today's meeting went well, perhaps she'd mention something to Captain Archer.

The four men rose at once in a display of split-second, well-coordinated courtesy. The oldest of them—the one Hoshi assumed was in charge—nodded to an empty chair beside him.

"Ma'am," he said politely.

Hoshi was both charmed and a bit taken aback by the combination of chivalry and stiff formality. She sat.

As if they'd been practicing the move for months, the soldiers retook their seats in flawless unison. *Whump.*

None of them picked up their silverware, but instead waited for Hoshi to make the first move. The one who'd spoken appeared to be near forty; the others were much younger, but all of them were fit, chiseled, and flawlessly groomed. The mottled gray camos were spotless.

"I'm Hoshi Sato," she said.

"We've familiarized ourselves with all the bridge officers, Ensign," the older man replied. "I'm Major Hayes. This is Sergeant Kemper, Corporals Romero and Chang." He nodded at the different men in turn. Each favored Hoshi with a polite but reserved nod. They seemed friendly enough, but it was clear that they were a bit taken aback by the attempts of a crew member to fraternize with them.

Hoshi tried to think of a topic of conversation, and at last noticed that all the soldiers' plates were heaped high with food. They'd apparently just sat down, and were getting ready to dig in. She lifted her fork—and immediately the MACOs began shoveling in lunch with a speed and efficiency that was astonishing.

She nodded at Romero's plate. "Looks like you've all gotten your space legs."

Kemper, a ruddy-faced blond, grinned and shared an amused look with Romero. Spacesickness had definitely been an issue for them, and some kind of running joke. He finished chewing the huge mouthful of food he'd taken and swallowed. "Some of us are still visiting Dr. Phlox every morning."

Romero rolled his eyes at the memory of more unpleasant moments. "Wonders of modern medicine."

Hoshi was pleased; the conversational ball was rolling. She turned to the blond MACO. "What do you think of our doctor, Sergeant? I imagine you don't run into many Denobulans in Canton, Ohio."

The soldiers all reacted with surprise; at first, Hoshi didn't understand why. She had such an ear for dialect that she hadn't even realized she'd mentioned Canton. She wasn't trying to show off—it was just that she'd written a dissertation on the Midwestern "o"—long and round, with its Scandinavian influence.

"Actually, I'm stationed outside of Atlanta," Kemper said. He was a little taken aback. "No Denobulans, but we have our fair share of alien visitors." He paused, forkful of food hovering an inch from his mouth, then said, "You must've gone pretty deep into our records. I haven't lived in Ohio since junior high school."

Great, Hoshi thought, *now they think I've been prying.* She smiled again and explained, "You may have left Canton, but you've still got plenty of Canton left in your inflections."

Kemper frowned, puzzled. "Excuse me?"

Inflections—not a common term, except for someone in her profession. Hoshi tried to think of an alternative word, and was stumped.

Fortunately, Major Hayes saved the day. Bemused, he paused in his voracious eating long enough to say, "Ensign Sato's a linguist, Kemper. Give her enough time, she could probably tell you what street you grew up on."

Kemper's guarded expression turned into one of respect. Corporal Chang, slender and brown-skinned, with delicate features that no doubt belied his physical strength, asked softly, "Do you have any idea where we're headed, Ensign?"

Hoshi was now at a true loss. As an ensign, it was not her place to give out such information unless she was ordered to do so. In her best effort at tact, she said, "I'm sure Captain Archer will let us know when he has reason to."

Major Hayes suddenly became all business. "Let's hope it's soon," he said, his tone flinty. "The quicker *you* folks find these Xindi, the quicker *we* can get to work."

He rose abruptly; Hoshi glanced down and saw, to her astonishment, that his plate was completely empty.

The others rose a mere half-second after their commander—once again, in unison.

"Ma'am," Hayes said.

The four of them moved swiftly to the door.

Hoshi watched them go with a sense of disappointment: this was not going to be as easy as she anticipated. They were suffering, just like every *Enterprise* crew member, from a sense of frustration because of the waiting. Even more disturbing, they seemed to think that *they* were the real ones in charge of the mission; the *Enterprise* was simply providing the ride.

Hoshi sighed and began to eat her curry—extra hot, the way she liked it. Captain Archer—and Lieutenant Reed, especially—weren't going to appreciate the MACOs' attitude. She sensed trouble brewing, but had no idea how to stop it.

*   *   *

In one of the lower level corridors, Trip Tucker and Captain Archer were on the move.

Trip forced himself to try to attain his usual sense of alertness, of focus on the task at hand. It was impossible, but he did a fairly good job of going through the motions.

He loved his job, he told himself. Loved being in space. Now that the stakes had risen, and they were in the Expanse, he had a chance to truly make a difference, to be a part of saving Earth.

The Earth that was left, anyway. But not the Earth he'd known: Lizzie was gone from it.

So he went through his daily routine, staying busy, but it was like moving through molasses. Doctor Phlox had given him something to help him sleep, but he wanted more of it than the doc was willing to give him: He wanted to blot out every dream, every thought of Lizzie and her cruel death until there was nothing but blackness.

He'd thought, once they'd entered the Expanse, that things would happen quickly: there'd be danger, fighting, a chance to finally wreak revenge on the Xindi, which Trip was convinced would bring him peace. But it hadn't happened. They'd been hurtling through space forever, until Trip at last grew so exhausted from his grief that he settled into a dull numbness—except when he was alone, when the pain sometimes broke through with breathtaking force.

As he moved through the corridor with Archer, how-ever, Trip was all business. He liked to think that, though the loss of Lizzie accompanied him everywhere, a silent ghost, no one else saw.

"Just Bay Two?" Archer interrupted Trip's reverie. Like Trip, Archer had kept to himself during these unbearably slow weeks; neither of them had felt up to continuing their habit of socializing with each other. Trip didn't envy the Captain his responsibility: It was one thing to lose a sister, quite another to bear responsibility for the fate of nearly a hundred people.

"Yes, sir," Trip answered smartly, proud of his ability to draw himself out of his private thoughts quickly now. He had to do so, if he was going to be any good at help-ing to bring the Xindi to justice. "Cargo Bays One and Three seem to be unaffected."

"When did it start?"

"About ten minutes ago," Trip replied. "Ensign McFarlane got pretty banged up, but he's gonna be okay." Trip had been terrified at the sight of McFarlane, helpless, being crushed against the wall by a huge cargo container—terrified not just for the ensign, but also in a selfish way. He couldn't handle the thought of losing a man under his watch—not now. One death was enough—more than enough—to deal with. He'd rushed McFarlane to sickbay himself, and had been enor-mously gratified when Doctor Phlox pronounced the in-juries minor.

"And you're sure it's not a problem with the grav-plating?" Archer glanced at him. Like Trip, the Captain seemed grateful for a distraction, a problem, anything to ease the waiting.

Trip shook his head; the grav-plating had been the first thing he'd checked, but even then he'd known that the sort of poltergeist activities that had injured McFarlane couldn't be caused by defective grav-plating. Floating containers, yes. But not *this* . . .

The two men reached the doors leading to Cargo Bay Two. Trip paused for drama's sake, then tapped the control.

The doors slid open; Trip and the Captain entered the vast, silent chamber.

Just as Trip knew it would, Archer's expression grew puzzled as he stared at the empty bay floor. It was, of course, supposed to be loaded with stacked cargo.

Trip watched as Archer gazed, curious, to the left, then to the right—where the cargo was currently glued to the right bulkhead, all the way from floor to ceiling.

Startled by the sight, Archer took a step forward; Trip held up a restraining arm.

"Careful, sir. Stay close to the door."

Archer stepped back, and shot a questioning look at his engineer.

"Just give it a minute," Trip said.

They waited. After a beat, a low rumble began to build, growing louder and louder; the deck beneath their feet began to vibrate. With a sudden roar, the cargo containers whipped across the room, then slammed into place on the left-hand wall.

In a matter of seconds, the entire load of cargo had shifted to the opposite bulkhead. Abruptly, the deck ceased shaking, and all fell silent.

Archer drew back, suitably impressed. "You're right," he said. "It's not the grav-plating." A note of concern crept into his tone. "Is there any volatile material in those containers?"

Trip shook his head. That had occurred to him as well; he'd pulled the records, but common sense had already dictated his answer, which he gave the Captain now. "We would've known by now."

Archer stared at the containers, firmly held in place on the left bulkhead by some cock-eyed rendition of gravity, and considered them a moment. At last, he made a sweeping gesture at the bay with his chin. "Seal it off." He turned to go, then paused. "Let's hope this little 'anomaly' doesn't last any longer than the others did."

He strode off, leaving Trip to ponder the event. Tucker lingered until the deck began to rumble again, and watched with an engineer's delight as the cargo containers went flying from the left bulkhead to the right, then snapping into place, held fast by an invisible force.

It was a miracle McFarlane hadn't been killed.

Trip knew that the Captain was trying to follow a lead—a rumor, really—to a mining colony where there *might* be a Xindi. He hadn't permitted himself to think much about it, at least not while he was on duty; but for the first time, he considered how Archer must be feeling about the situation. If Trip had been so horrified at the thought of losing McFarlane, how must the Captain react to the notion of bringing his people closer to unknown danger?

Perhaps, Trip decided, he was being selfish, grieving so for Lizzie, when there were so many other people who had suffered, were suffering, as a result of the attack on Earth.

He drew in a deep breath and tried to break free from the numbness, the thickly veiled pain, and failed.

T'Pol entered sickbay to find Phlox staring at a monitor connected to his neutron microscope; beside him on the counter sat several Petri dishes filled with active cultures.

Whatever the Doctor was looking at, it pleased him immensely, for he was indulging in one of his intense Denobulan grins.

When T'Pol stepped up beside him, Phlox's smile widened impossibly; he turned to her and gestured with enthusiasm at the display on the screen.

"Come, look at this! The pigmentation is far more colorful than I would've suspected."

While T'Pol did not share the doctor's emotionality, she could appreciate his unalloyed enjoyment of science. She gazed at the monitor. Clearly, these were some sort of living dermal cells—hard and glistening, like the skin of Terran snakes, and aesthetically quite pleasing. Each shimmered with translucent, warm jewel-tone colors, from topaz to crimson, with hints of citrine.

"What are we looking at?" she asked. With Phlox, always researching and testing new medical alternatives, it was impossible to deduce.

"Xindi epithelial cells," Phlox replied with satisfaction. "I've been transnucleating the tissue samples harvested from the corpse they found inside the crashed probe."

"It looks more like scales," T'Pol remarked.

"Precisely," Phlox agreed, nodding in his perpetually cheerful manner. "When I'm finished constructing my physiometric profile, I wouldn't be surprised if he turns out to have reptilian characteristics."

She had thought Phlox had called her to sickbay in order to consult her about what he had just shown her; it was clear now that he was indulging in one of his more roundabout behaviors. He had engaged her in conversation about something else in order to broach a more difficult subject. While the tactic was no doubt useful for putting humans at ease, T'Pol preferred to get directly to the point.

"You wanted to see me?" she asked.

Phlox picked up the next Petri dish from the counter and began to prepare it for the microscope. His smile vanished; his manner grew uncharacteristically serious. "Do you have any siblings?"

A Vulcan would consider this a personal question, but T'Pol answered it directly, even though she did not see what possible need the doctor would have for such information. "No."

"Commander Tucker had one sister," Phlox said softly. "She was killed in the attack."

T'Pol remembered the expression on the Commander's face shortly after the event, when she had encountered him in Captain Archer's ready room. The pain in his eyes had been raw, the anger almost feral when T'Pol had brought news of the crashed spaceship. Tucker had demanded concerning the pilot, *Who the hell was he? What species?*

She had thought then of Vulcan history, of the savagery; of an ancient cave painting of a warrior who had shared the same burning look in his eyes. Until that day in the ready room, T'Pol had never seen in person the emotions that led to revenge.

"I'm aware of that," she told Phlox.

' "He's having difficulty dealing with the loss," the doctor confided, in a tone that conveyed admirable compassion.

"That's to be expected," T'Pol said. She had never experienced a violent death in her immediate family; even so, a Vulcan would deal with such a tragedy with far more equanimity. Humans—perhaps because they were shorter-lived, perhaps because of their philosophy—possessed a fear of death she had never understood, which was no doubt why they grieved more for their loved ones.

"More specifically," Phlox added, slowly inching closer to the point, "it's affecting his sleep. I've been giving him sedatives, but I'd like to see him start tapering off."

He paused, leaving T'Pol uncertain; such a matter was between a patient and his physician. She did not see how she needed to be involved. "I'm not sure I understand."

Phlox drew a breath, then at last stated his reason in calling T'Pol to sickbay. "I believe the Commander would be a fine candidate for Vulcan neuropressure."

The Doctor's reluctance to state his objective immediately suddenly made complete sense; the application of neuropressure required a great degree of physical contact—and the partial disrobing of the patient. Because of its exceptionally personal nature, it was not something Vulcans were eager to do—even for each other, much less a human.

In an effort to be diplomatic, T'Pol did not refuse the request outright. "I doubt the Commander would have the patience to sit in one place long enough to get through the first posture."

"I'm certain with your delicate guidance . . ." Phlox coaxed, his gaze one of pure charm. The Denobulan, T'Pol decided, would have made an excellent diplomat.

Flatly, she countered, *Delicate* is not a word I associate with Mister Tucker."

The Doctor merely continued to look at her with his frank, open gaze. Words were unnecessary; he was thinking only of Commander Tucker's good, and giving T'Pol time to contemplate that fact.

The situation was hardly comfortable; T'Pol tried to explain her point of view, although she already sensed that hers was a losing battle. "The instruction of neuropressure is a very intimate act."

Phlox's expression showed that he was already well aware of the fact. "And he's suffered a very intimate loss. He needs your help."

T'Pol stood silently and considered this. If Commander Tucker truly needed her help, then she was ethically bound to supply it, regardless of the personal discomfort it might cause her. In fact, logic demanded she do so: Tucker was critical to their mission, therefore his well-being was of vital importance.

She let go an inaudible sigh and gazed at Phlox, who was leaning forward expectantly. "Have him come to my quarters at twenty-two hundred hours."

She turned and headed for the door; Phlox's voice stopped her.

"There's one little problem," the Doctor said, in a way that made T'Pol believe her level of discomfort was about to rise even more. She turned to face him.

Phlox's expression was a bit wry. "Assuming that you'd agree to my request, I suggested all this to Commander Tucker earlier today."

Motionless, T'Pol waited.

"He was . . ."—Phlox paused, searching for the right words—". . . less than enthusiastic."

Clearly, the Doctor was expecting something else from her, but T'Pol could not deduce what he was hinting at. "I don't understand," she said.

"Perhaps if I could get him to go to your quarters tonight . . . say twenty-two hundred hours . . . you might be able to convince him of the lasting benefits of Vulcan neuropressure."

So: she was now called upon not only to engage in an activity with Commander Tucker that required a distasteful degree of personal contact, she was also expected to cooperate in deceiving him.

For an instant, she considered lecturing Phlox about Vulcan ethics and honesty—but then the memory of her uniform, still hanging in her closet, returned to her.

She had chosen to go to the Expanse, to help the inhabitants of Earth; now was not the time to indulge in self-righteousness.

She returned Phlox's hopeful gaze with something less than enthusiasm; he had known all along, of course, that she would not logically or ethically be able to refuse his request, despite her reluctance.

Flatly, she said, "Good night, Doctor."

Phlox understood the response for the capitulation it was. T'Pol turned and exited, leaving him to smile brilliantly behind her.

Chapter 11

Deep beneath the surface of a planet whose name she did not know, the miner Xelia shuffled, feet and shoulders aching, through the dark, narrow tunnel toward another mindless day's work.

Or perhaps it was night; she could not see. It had been a full ten solar revolutions, according to her homeworld's way of reckoning time, since she had last seen the sun of this planet she merely thought of as Blue. Blue was the color of the toxic haze through which she now walked, queued up with six fellow miners; all of their faces were swaddled against the hazardous fumes, revealing only their streaming, stinging eyes. That was all Xelia knew of her peers—their eyes, for they were not allowed to speak with each other during work time, and too exhausted after to do more than eat and sleep.

Blue was the color of the poisonous trellium they mined; it caked the walls dark cobalt; it stained Xelia's nails, colored her hair, her boil-covered skin—and, she knew, despite the pathetic protection afforded by the rag, her lungs.

By now, her brain was blue as well. She knew she was entering the last stages of trellium poisoning; she coughed blue-black sputum constantly onto her rags, and listened to her breath come and go in rasps. There were times, at night, when she bolted from sleep, struggling for air, feeling as though one of the great monsters that served as guards were sitting upon her chest.

Xelia did not fear the thought of death; it would come as a relief. But she feared dying. She had seen other miners go before her, and she knew the end was painful, with convulsions and gasping; she had heard the cries, all the more pitiful because they were incoherent. Trellium destroyed not only the mucosal lining of the throat and mouth, garbling speech, it also brought a fatal dementia. She had seen fellow workers hurl away their tools, tear away their rags, and bellow—only to be shot down by the guards.

The first sign was loss of memory—and Xelia struggled during the agonizing, tedious days trying to remember her homeworld, her life before the hellish mines.

Roa—Roja—She could remember only the beginning of her home planet's name. She clung to it fiercely, repeating it to herself at night in a croak of a voice she could no longer recognize as her own. How had she come to be here? She had been young, a beautiful female, not yet mated. She was still young, though the mines had transformed her into a hideous, dying creature. A freighter; she had worked aboard a freighter, and there had been a distress signal from the planet of Blue . . . She tried, and failed, to recall those who had served with her aboard the freighter. All of them had long since perished.

Xelia filed with the other miners past twelve guards, each one her full height plus half. They stood, menacing towers, over their piteous charges, clutching large weapons that glowed in the dark cyan haze. Their race was alien to her; like her peers, they never revealed their faces, which remained covered by rebreathers; to Xelia, the rebreathers looked like great, tentacled parasites. She imagined them sucking the brains from the guards; certainly, they could not be highly intelligent to have chosen such a profession. Perhaps, she thought, they didn't even have faces.

Or perhaps they, too, were like her, unwilling victims forced into service.

A voice, rasping and breathless, suddenly crackled through the overhead com and echoed through the long, narrow corridors.

"Emergency crews to Level Sixteen! There's been a collapse in the secondary access shaft!"

Xelia turned with the others and began running away from the catacomb of tunnels, toward safety. As she did, one of the guards struck her shoulder with his rifle, propelling her forward faster. She cried out; the sound was animallike, unrecognizable to her own ears.

The com voice continued over the sounds of panic.

"Protecting the trellium flow must take precedence over any rescue attempts!"

Miners would be left to die, Xelia knew. The lucky ones would perish almost immediately from the trauma of being crushed beneath layers of bulwark and trellium; others, knowing no action would be taken to save them, would be left to suffocate over a matter of a few hours.

Xelia envied them all. She only wished she had the courage to turn and run—not away from the disaster, but into the very heart of it.

Several meters above her on the planet surface, the foreman of the mining complex stood in his dark office, lit only by an oil lamp and two flickering monitors covered with blue soot and grime. His name was Baloran, and he, too, had not seen the sun for several years. The planet's surface had long ago turned into a wind-blown desert, its natural sky blotted out by thick blue clouds composed of trellium particulates. If there was a name for the planet, Baloran had never learned it either; the world he and his business cohorts raped for its main resource was inconsequential. He never referred to it, only to the mining complex itself as the Base.

At the moment, Baloran was still shouting—as best his damaged lungs permitted him—into the filthy com unit that hung from the ceiling of his office.

"Production must not be delayed!"

On the last syllable, his voice cracked; he let go the microphone, which automatically ascended back to the ceiling. Baloran leaned forward, hands on thighs, and coughed until he very nearly retched, then swiped an inhaler from his desk and sucked in a deep breath.

The tightness in his throat and lungs eased immediately; grateful, he drew in another breath, then scratched at the boils on his neck and jawline.

Damned nasty place to work. The trellium got into everything, despite what his superiors told him. *Minor irritation,* the man who'd hired him had said. *You'll get used to it.*

It was all a lie, of course; it wasn't until Baloran got to the Base that he'd seen just how toxic trellium was. Even his fingernails were stained a permanent blue now. The others had all told him to wear a rebreather, but he'd refused it. *I don't need that thing—I won't be here all that long. Besides, I'm tough. Got good lungs.*

He was too embarrassed to admit the very thought of putting a rebreather on his face made him shake with claustrophobia. He'd put in his time, then take the money—good pay it was—and get out.

Behind him, the metal door clanged open; he turned to see the head guard enter.

Baloran was no good with names. The head guard was named something like "Xathar" or "Xaran," but Baloran gave up trying to remember and instead just avoided addressing him altogether. He hadn't bothered to learn about the guards' species, either; he wasn't here to make extraterrestrial friends, just to make some money. All he knew was that they were tall bruisers, and he had no desire to mess with them.

Fortunately, they had a well-developed sense of hierarchy, and treated Baloran with respect. Even now, the huge alien bowed slightly and said, with an officious air, "The starship's entered orbit. They've asked to see you."

Baloran set the inhaler down and smiled faintly.

"Send them our coordinates," he said.

If he hadn't had the scanners to tell him otherwise, Archer would have thought the foreman had given him the wrong coordinates; as the Captain maneuvered the shuttlepod down toward the planet's surface, he had absolutely no visual of the mining complex until he was right on top of it. Swirling, murky blue clouds hid the two towers until the pod, with Archer and Reed inside, slowly descended beside them.

The towers were massive old structures, of dull, worn metal, pitted by the corrosive gases and particulate matter hurled about by the gale-force winds. Dozens of vents on the towers' roofs and flanks constantly belched plumes of dark blue smoke, which was immediately seized and drawn upward by the violent air currents.

It was a less than welcoming sight, but Archer did not permit himself an instant's hesitation before opening the pod hatch and stepping out into the maelstrom. Reed, his demeanor only slightly more tentative, followed.

Immediately, Archer threw up his hands to shield his eyes, and fought to steady his stance. The wind was blowing nearly sideways, pelting him with a fine grit that stung eyes and skin. The smell surprised him: he came from a world and time unused to the stench of toxic chemicals. His eyes and nose both began to run.

Despite the surprise, he got his bearings quickly enough; he had important work to do here, critical work, and every second's hesitation was another second given the Xindi to develop the weapon that would destroy Earth. Cupping a hand over his eyes to shield them, Archer oriented himself to the towers—imminently close, yet ghostly even in this distance, due to the thick, murky haze—and began making his way toward his destination.

It was slow going; the surface was a layer of soft, fine grit, like powdery beach sand, and they were walking into the wind. Over its howl, Archer could hear the roar of machinery. As he trudged toward the nearest tower, head ducked to protect his eyes and face, Reed screamed next to him, "We should've worn EV suits!"

Archer faced Reed so he could be heard and shouted back, "The Doctor said it was safe for short periods!" Phlox had explained that trellium (an element Archer'd never heard of) was the main component, fatal when breathed in directly over months or years. But brief, limited exposure required only a simple detox procedure, with no harm done.

Eyes reduced to slits, face contorted in a grimace, Reed challenged, "Safe? You call this safe? I've been in—"

He broke off, gagging—caught a mouthful of grit, Archer imagined—and started coughing.

The Captain gave him a quick slap on the back, then ordered, "Try not to talk!"

Reed nodded, speechless.

After a long, miserable moment, they reached the first tower. Archer had memorized the foreman's directions, and found the ladder he'd described—although it was far rustier and more unsteady-looking than the Captain had imagined. He caught hold of it gingerly and began climbing up. Once again, Reed followed, until the two of them made their way to a platform.

Archer unbolted a metal door, per the foreman's instructions; it opened onto a dark, spiraling stairwell that led downwards.

The Captain went first. Getting out of the wind and stinging sand was a relief—but descending the rickety metal staircase was hardly an aesthetic experience. The walls and stairs wore a thick coat of dark blue mineral residue, and the air still bore a noxious chemical stink, mixed now with the odor of the sweat and filth of living bodies. Even here, a deep blue haze hung suspended; Archer was beginning to agree with Reed about those EV suits. A respirator would do nicely, helping to ease the burning that was starting to spread from the Captain's nose and throat into his lungs.

Now that the howling wind was no longer in their ears, the relentless churning of machinery was more noticeable; it caused the metal beneath Archer's soles to vibrate. Hard to tell, given the haze, but it seemed to him even the walls trembled.

They kept going down . . . down, down until Archer's calves began to cramp, until he began to wonder whether he had somehow misunderstood part of what the foreman had told him.

Finally, he heard Reed's footsteps behind him stop; Archer turned to regard the Lieutenant, then followed his gaze down the stairwell.

It descended, apparently, into infinity.

Archer began moving again, and Reed followed. But the Lieutenant's brow, coated with fine blue dust, was furrowed with uncertainty. "There has to be at least two hundred—"

Archer stopped in his tracks as two great, hulking figures—aliens of a sort Archer had never seen before—appeared in the cobalt haze, standing before him. Despite the dim light, he did not miss the fact that they each bore large weapons in the crooks of their arms.

Archer was, of course, startled, but recovered at once. These were no doubt the assistants the foreman had mentioned. Pretty formidable-looking ones, but Archer wasn't about to let himself be intimidated. "I'm Captain Archer of the *Starship Enterprise*," he announced confidently. "We've come to see—"

One of the guards interrupted him, in the deepest bass Archer'd ever heard. "This way."

The aliens turned without pleasantry and abruptly headed down the winding stairs. Archer shot Reed a long-suffering glance.

There was something about the situation—maybe the

fact that the assistants were enormous and armed, as if they were soldiers rather than workers—that set off an instinctive alarm in Archer's brain. Something didn't smell right . . . and it wasn't just the trellium.

The quartet descended several more levels before the aliens finally moved away from the stairs, toward a large metal door where three more tall aliens of the same species stood watch—again, all of them armed.

Archer was growing more distrustful by the minute. Why would a foreman of a bunch of miners need guards? This planet was definitely not in a busy neighborhood; were pirates that much of a problem—or was the situation not what he'd been told?

He and Reed were led into a grease- and trellium-covered room that was as dismal as the rest of the complex; the guards exited and shut the door behind them with a loud clang.

It was then Archer noticed the slight, hunch-shouldered foreman, reduced to a dark silhouette in the blue haze. Behind him, a primitive oil-lamp flickered, casting shadows that intermittently hid his face. Archer caught just enough of his sly expression and cold, glittering eyes to think, *weasel*, and know for certain that his instincts were right: He was dealing with a con artist.

An uneasy silence passed as the weasel studied the two officers, then drew in air with a rattling in his lungs and let go a single, rasping sound. "Archer."

"I'm Jonathan Archer," the Captain said, without

warmth, and stepped forward. He gestured with his chin. "This is Lieutenant Reed."

In the dimness, the foreman smiled unctuously and scratched at some nasty boils on his stubbled chin. "I was told you might make it worth my while if I were to arrange a certain introduction."

Archer kept his tone hard. "It depends on what you mean by 'worth your while.' "

The foreman tilted his long, gaunt face and showed long, yellowed teeth. "I've always had a fondness for platinum . . . specifically in its liquified state."

"I'm afraid we don't carry precious metals on board."

"A pity." The foreman turned dismissively from him, and moved as if to summon the "assistants." His manner made it clear that negotiation was not an option.

Archer at once turned mollifying. "I'm sure there's something else we could offer you . . ."

The weasel whirled on him, wheezing with fury. "I don't make a habit of allowing people to interrupt my workers! Xindi or otherwise!"

Xindi.

A thrill ran down Archer's spine at the very mention of the word. So it wasn't just a rumor; there *was* a Xindi here, now. He fought not to let the desperation show on his face. Instead, he sidled closer to Reed and said in the Lieutenant's ear, "What about the antimatter relays?"

Reed replied in a voice barely audible above the machinery's hum. "Their linings are plated with a platinum-cobalt alloy. Trip could probably strip them down and separate the metals."

Archer directed his full attention to the foreman; the Captain's manner was all business. "How much platinum are we talking about?"

The foreman's temper cooled immediately; the smirk returned. "I'm a reasonable man. I'm sure you could part with a half liter."

"I'll need to see this man," Archer said, "scan him . . . confirm that he's Xindi."

The foreman's smile widened. He moved to a desk, pulled open a filthy drawer, and removed a darkly stained piece of cloth. He held it up so the other two men could see. "That won't be necessary."

He handed the cloth to Archer—who unwrapped it, and recoiled slightly at the sight of a swollen humanoid finger, severed below the second knuckle. A jagged ivory metatarsal protruded from bloodied purplish flaps of skin.

Archer glared at the foreman in pure disgust. "Why would you do this?"

"An unfortunate accident," the weasel said glibly. His tone turned dismissive. "I'll expect to see you back tomorrow. Good day."

With a wiry arm, he lifted a metal pipe from his desk and rapped against the wall.

A moment later, one of the vertiginously tall "assistants" opened the door; Archer and Reed followed him out into the blue glow.

* * *

It was a bright blue day at the Key West Café—one of those gloriously pleasant days in March, a month before the humidity took hold and the sun grew so hot that every afternoon brought a tropical shower.

Lizzie was sitting outside—she always liked to sit outside at the Café, even when it was too warm—reading a book, the way she did when she had to eat alone. She was wearing that blue sundress, the one with the little shoulderstraps, and her blond hair fell straight onto her shoulders. How old was she? Eight . . . Yeah, eight, the year when she was on the grilled-cheese sandwich kick. It was all she would eat at the Café, Swiss please, not cheddar, with extra pickles on the side. Mom had said if Lizzie didn't start eating something else, she was going to start sprouting holes.

Trip was standing across the street, next to the lime grove owned by old man Farley, flanked by two huge, fuschia-colored hibiscus. He was wearing his favorite shirt, a geometric display of rust, gold, and olive. And he was worried—shouting at Lizzie, but for some reason, he couldn't project his voice, couldn't yell loud enough to be heard.

So she just went right on reading her book, blissfully unawares; she frowned, wrinkling her freckled nose in that little-girl way she had, and turned the page as she took another bite of her cheese sandwich. Slowly, pensively, she chewed.

"Elizabeth!" Trip screamed, waving his arms. "Lizzie!"

He looked, and the Café was suddenly filled with adults. Only Lizzie sat alone, still reading and chewing her sandwich, still oblivious.

Trip was gesticulating wildly now, his adolescent voice cracking. "Lizzie! You've got to get out of there!"

And there was Lizzie suddenly in her twenties, still sitting at the same table in the same crowd, eating the same sandwich, reading the same book, still dressed in the blue sundress, her blonde, sun-streaked hair still long and straight.

"Elizabeth!" Trip yelled, his voice and body now adult, his shirt the same melange of rust, gold, and green. Panic overtook him; despite the sun's warmth, a cold sweat trickled down his spine, soaking the lightweight shirt. "Please!! Get out of there! YOU'VE GOTTA GET OUT OF THERE!"

The grown-up Lizzie was abruptly alone, abandoned, but still accompanied by her lunch and book.

Miracle of miracles, she looked up directly at Trip and smiled dazzlingly.

Trip screamed, his throat raw from the effort, but no sound came from his mouth.

"LISTEN TO ME!! YOU'VE GOT TO GET AWAY!!"

Lizzie smiled and began to wave.

Behind her, the entire sky had become a swath of flame . . . moving directly toward her.

Trip sobbed with horror, trying to scream, trying to be heard, but Lizzie merely continued smiling and waving, happy to see her brother, unmindful of the coming danger.

The incinerating beam swept closer, closer, until it was on top of her. . . .

Trip woke gasping with terror, then pressed his palms to his eyes; when he at last drew his hands away, they were damp, shaking.

It's all right, his mind chattered inanely. *Just a dream. Just a dream . . . It's probably just because you know the Captain and Reed are on the trail of the Xindi. . . .*

But it *wasn't* all right. Trip had roughly the same dream every night, though the circumstances varied. One night, Lizzie would be eating at her favorite restaurant, the next, working in her office, and even once watching a film at the old movie theater.

Grief was a strange thing: Trip was beginning to understand what Reed had been trying to say about closure, about a way of saying good-bye—but the Xindi had taken that away.

Because even if the Xindi were stopped, even if Trip managed to feel that some measure of justice had been done, there would always be one fact that would forever haunt him: He would never know exactly how Lizzie had died.

Chapter 12

In sickbay, Phlox was presenting the results of his findings to Captain Archer.

Humans were curious creatures; Phlox found them fascinating, especially in terms of their complex emotional reactions to events. He found that he had to temper his enthusiasm for science when around them, especially the Captain, who of late only wanted to hear the information he needed that would help him locate the Xindi. Then there was Lieutenant Trip, of course, and his difficulties concerning the loss of his sister. While Denobulans grieved the loss of a loved one, they did not discriminate between different *types* of grief, the way humans did: For example, Phlox would mourn the peaceful passing of an elderly relative in precisely the same manner he would mourn the traumatic death of a younger one: dying was dying.

And the doctor was just beginning to wonder whether

he should be concerned about the state of Archer's mental health: the Captain was beginning to hyperfocus on the Xindi. This was necessary—to an extent. But he had noted that Archer had entirely given up socializing with other crew members, and was no longer checking out books from the ship's library. While the success of the mission was extremely critical, so was the Captain's mental health.

As Archer stood nearby, watching Phlox manipulate the microscope's controls, the doctor reminded himself to keep things brief.

Even so, as he brought up the display of alien cells on the monitor so the Captain could view them, Phlox couldn't help making at wry face at the severed finger. It sat exposed on a tray beside the delicate scalpels used to, obtain micrometer-thin slices.

"A blood sample would've been sufficient," the doctor remarked. "Some saliva . . ."

Archer, ever intense, demanded, "Is it Xindi?"

Phlox wanted to be direct, but he first had to be honest. "Yes . . . and no."

The Captain scowled. "I need something a little more concrete, Doctor."

Phlox explained. "The genetic profile is nearly identical to the tissue samples taken from the corpse found on Earth. . . . Their base-pair sequencing is far closer than, say, humans and chimpanzees. *Nearly* identical, but not quite."

Archer contemplated this. "Like humans and Neanderthals?"

"A reasonable analogy." Phlox moved to a nearby monitor and pressed a control, causing a three-dimensional model of an alien humanoid to rotate slowly on the screen. "After analyzing the skeletal remains of the Xindi corpse," he said, "and the tissue samples I was given, I was able to provide the computer with enough data to create this rendering." He nodded at the alien face displayed before them, with its slit-like nostrils and fine, gleaming scales. "However, *this* humanoid is reptilian . . . that finger"—he inclined his head toward the tray—"is not. It's covered with *skin*, not unlike yours or mine. But it's Xindi all the same."

Archer's expression grew pensive; at the same time, Phlox noted a slight glimmer of fascination, an echo of the excitement he, the doctor, had felt upon making such a discovery. On most of the planets discovered so far, the mammals had been the ones to evolve intelligence; more rarely, the reptilians had succeeded. But he had never heard before of a world where *both* groups had achieved ascendancy at the same time.

"I wish I could be more helpful, Captain," Phlox said, just as Commander Tucker entered the room. The doctor had no doubt as to the Commander's purpose here.

Archer gave a distracted nod, then turned to Tucker. "How's it coming?"

Tucker released the sigh of an engineer who had been ordered to do something *not* in the best interests of his engines. "We're gonna end up stripping more than two hundred relays to get half a liter of liquified platinum, but you'll have it by this afternoon."

"Let me know when it's ready," Archer said, already preoccupied with other matters. He headed for the door—then stopped, emerging from his reverie long enough to realize that his commander had just walked into sickbay.

"You okay?" he asked Tucker.

Tucker nodded and gave a dismissive little shrug; Phlox suspected he was too embarrassed to discuss the matter with Archer. "Yeah, fine."

The Captain did not press; he gave a nod, then left the Commander alone with Phlox.

The instant Archer was out of earshot, Tucker said, "I think I'm gonna need something to help me sleep tonight, Doc."

Phlox feigned a moment of contemplation, then said, "Very well. Come by at around twenty-two hundred hours. I'll see what I can do."

"Thanks," Trip said. Phlox detected the undercurrent of weariness in his tone; the pigmentation beneath his eyes had darkened slightly over the past few days. Clearly, he'd had some difficult nights.

The doctor watched him go. As difficult as the situation might be for T'Pol, Phlox knew her to be possessed of great compassion, and an unusual intuitive capacity, for a Vulcan, to understand humans. He had faith that she would be able to overcome her cultural reluctance and help Commander Tucker.

If a human ever needed a Vulcan's help, the Commander needed it now.

*   *   *

Inside the dim, hazy foreman's office, Archer stood beside the weaselly little man and watched as Trip Tucker placed a large metallic suitcase on the filthy wasteland of a desk and snapped it open.

Archer did not like the acrid, toxic blue surroundings, or the muscular alien giants who waited just outside the door, weapons in hand, nor did he like the growing sense that he was at a disadvantage here. Most of all, he disliked the foreman, who scratched unconsciously at his chin and neck, now so covered with boils so inflamed the redness could be detected beneath the veil of blue soot he wore.

Trip had insisted on coming. He was, after all, the most experienced engineer and had designed the container for holding the ultra-unstable precious metal; but Archer figured he had the most right anyway. There was a Xindi involved—and the Captain realized how desperate Trip must be to do something, anything, to help prevent another attack on Earth.

On the way down in the shuttlepod, Tucker had fallen grimly silent; his reticent mood persisted until they finally arrived at their destination, at which point he became suddenly animated, relieved that something was finally happening after all these weeks.

Now, bent over the foreman's desk, Trip removed a thickly insulated container with consummate delicacy, set it down, then gently released a locking mechanism. Using one hand to hold the container steady, he used the other to open the top, revealing what lay inside: a crystal vial filled with a glowing substance.

Quicksilver, Archer thought, but this was far more intense a substance; it was painfully, metallically white, so dazzling that when the Captain looked away, he saw the afterimage, superimposed against dull blue.

Trip glanced over his shoulder at the foreman, who was leering with pure greed at the contents of the suitcase. "I suppose you're aware this stuff is very volatile above thirty degrees Celsius."

The foreman was not interested in making eye contact with Trip; he continued to stare, mesmerized by the contents of the vial. "I'm very familiar with the properties of liquified platinum."

Trip gently replaced the top, then turned. "I've insulated the outer container . . . it should keep everything pretty stable."

Archer directed a pointed look at the wiry little foreman. "There's a little more than half a liter in there."

A real weasel, the Captain thought, looking at him. The man was actually rubbing his trellium-caked hands together; any minute now, and he'd begin to drool. "What exactly is it you want with our Xindi friend?" the foreman asked; his tone turned lascivious. "He's not very attractive . . . especially after his recent . . . surgery."

Archer regarded the man with unmasked disgust. His instincts about the weasel had been right. Not only was the man untrustworthy, he couldn't imagine someone else being capable of anything but the basest intentions.

He kept his tone short, clipped. "I have something I need to discuss with him."

"And what might that be?" Curious, the weasel leaned closer; Archer recoiled at the man's stench. Clearly, regular bathing wasn't one of his priorities.

None of your damned business, Archer wanted to say, but instead, he allowed himself an impatient: "You got what you asked for, now let me see the Xindi."

The foreman studied him for a half-second, as if considering whether to comply, then walked over to one of the dust-covered monitors. He ran a grimy hand over it, clearing away some of the blue grit but leaving behind oily fingerprints. He squinted at the readout for a moment.

"His work group should be awake in about an hour's time." He drew in a rattling breath and turned toward Archer and Tucker, his tone wheedling, smarmy. "Perhaps you'd like something to eat in the meanwhile?"

Archer let the flare of anger he felt come through in his tone. "It took six of my men half the night to extract that platinum. I think you could wake him up an hour early."

For the briefest instant, the weasel's glittering eyes flashed with equal ire. It faded swiftly, though, in a way that let Archer know he was at last about to set eyes on his first live Xindi.

They headed deep into the belly of the mines; the foreman led the way, accompanied, as always, by two armed guards.

When they finally made it into the miners' area, Archer's sense of foreboding increased. The passageways were narrow, the walls thickly caked with trellium residue, the tunnels filled with the thick blue murk that made Archer's eyes and throat burn; the smell was nauseating. What troubled him most were not the conditions, but the sight of the miners themselves—what Archer could see of them. They represented many different species, all of them dressed in tatters, all of them with faces wrapped in rags—save for the eyes.

The guards had elaborate breathing apparatuses, even though their exposure to trellium particulate matter was far less. Why would the miners tolerate such unsafe conditions?

And everywhere—everywhere Archer looked—there were armed guards.

They arrived at last in the miners' area—a labyrinth of tunnels and alcoves. The guards pushed open a thick metal door and led them all into the most primitive of living areas. Blue-tinged miners slept on the floor; some sat at rusty tables on uneven, rickety benches and ate. Even here, there were armed, musclebound aliens standing watch, as though a riot might suddenly break out.

Most remarkably, there was not a single sound—not the low murmur of voices, the lull of normal conversation. There was no social interaction at all, not even between members of the same species.

Trip sensed something was wrong, too. As the foreman

led them deeper back into the dimly lit, haze-filled work-ers' quarters, he shared a look with the Captain.

After a long pause, Trip finally asked, "Is trellium the only thing you mine here?"

"The only thing," the foreman responded, his tone cur-sory, his mind apparently on other things. "Trellium."

"I'm not familiar with it," Trip said. "What's it used for?"

"Insulation. Mostly for interstellar vessels." Inspiration suddenly struck the weasel; he turned to Archer, his ex-pression sly. "What sort of insulation does your ship use, Captain?"

Archer thought, and could see no possible harm in re-plying. "Our outer hull is lined with duranium."

The foreman's thin, blue lips began to curve in a coy little grin. "I imagine you have a very large crew."

Archer's tone turned sharp. "Why would you imagine that?" he asked, though he was beginning to suspect. No matter; he'd deal with that problem when it surfaced. In the interim, he had a Xindi to interview . . . assuming the foreman kept that much of his word.

Indeed, before the weasel managed to concoct another lie, one of the gargantuan aliens returned, his large paw gripping a human-sized miner. With a single thrust, he sent the miner hurtling forward; the humanoid collided with the nearest wall, sending up a fresh cloud of trel-lium dust, then sank to the floor.

The foreman, utterly unmoved by this display of bru-tality, told Archer casually, "Take your time." He headed, guards in tow, to the door.

Archer waited until he heard the metal door clang shut.

The instant it did, Trip bent down and helped the miner to his feet—a gesture not lost on Archer.

The miner—male, his body very humanoid in appearance, though his face was masked by rags—pulled angrily away from Trip. He held up a thickly bandaged hand.

His voice was deep and grating, though not as damaged as the foreman's. "Do I have you to thank for this?!" His words were muffled by the layer of rags that covered his nose and mouth.

It was not what Archer had expected of that first encounter: A Xindi angry at *him*. Mildly, he replied, "The foreman said it was an accident."

"Did he?" the alien answered snidely. He paused, eyeing the two humans with suspicion, then demanded, "What do you want?"

He did not, of course, know of the attack by his people on Earth: He had been in the mines too long, Archer realized. "You're Xindi?" the Captain asked.

"A nine-fingered Xindi," the humanoid allowed, with more than a little derision. "What do you want?"

"Where's your homeworld?"

The Xindi began pacing back and forth in front of Archer and Trip, sizing the Captain up. "You came all the way to this hideous planet . . . bribed the foreman to see me . . . for what, directions to my planet? I find that hard to believe."

"We have important business with your people." It was an honest enough answer.

The alien leaned forward, intrigued. "But you don't know where to find them." He considered this an instant, and apparently made a decision to trust Archer. Slowly, he unwound the cloths that covered mouth and nose, and at last revealed his face.

Archer heard Trip draw in a low breath beside him; it could not have been an easy moment for the engineer.

The Xindi was startlingly human in appearance. It would have been easier, Archer reflected, to hate him if he had looked radically different—but his appearance brought up an uncomfortable thought.

If we knew aliens were going to destroy Earth in the future, would we launch a weapon to destroy them first?

"If you want information," the Xindi said, "You're going to have to help me escape from this place."

"What do you mean escape?" Archer asked. He had already guessed the answer, but he wanted it verified.

The Xindi gestured at the pathetic, blue-stained creatures surrounding them. "Do these look like volunteers? We're captives—slaves!"

Archer exchanged a knowing look with Trip. To the Xindi, the Captain said, "A simple set of coordinates. That's all I want. I'm prepared to pay you."

There was an arrogance in the alien's voice that belied his desperate circumstance. "The only payment I'm interested in is my freedom. If you can't provide me with that, then stop wasting my time!"

Archer drew in a breath to reply, but stopped. Beside him came the softest sound: a low growl, emanating from deep within Trip Tucker's chest. In the space of less than a heartbeat, Archer watched as Trip struggled with a sudden burst of rage, then abruptly lost the battle.

The engineer surged forward and pegged the startled Xindi to the wall by the throat. In an instant, the two were nose-to-nose. Archer stood ready to intervene—but at the moment, he decided, a little shaking up might do the Xindi some good.

"I don't know what you're doing in this place, and I don't particularly care!" Trip proclaimed, with deadly heat. "But we didn't come here to stage a prison break, so why don't you just give us the coordinates and we'll *all* stop wasting each other's time!"

The Xindi glared at him, defiant. "Not until you get me off this planet!"

Face contorted in a sneer, Trip pulled the miner forward by the collar, then shoved him roughly back against the wall. "You know, I'm not sure why, but I'm just itching to kick the hell out of you."

Archer finally moved in and put a hand on his engineer's shoulder. "Trip, take it easy."

Tucker reluctantly loosened his grip, just as the Captain's communicator beeped.

Archer stepped aside and flipped it open. "Archer."

T'Pol's voice filtered through the grid. "Captain, there are three warships approaching at warp. Their hull alloys match the mining towers on the surface."

So, the weasel had been making plans all along, counting on a fresh supply of miners to replace those dying or dead from trellium exposure. "How long before they get here?" Archer asked.

The Vulcan's voice was replaced by Mayweather's. "Two hours, sir."

Archer pondered it for a second. "Go to Tactical Alert. We're heading back to the shuttlepod."

"Understood," T'Pol's disembodied voice replied.

Archer flipped his communicator closed.

"Shuttlepod?" the Xindi demanded. "You have a starship in orbit?"

Archer remained silent as he headed for the metal door. Trip and the Xindi followed.

"You've made it so easy for them!" the miner said, with a cruel delight that made it easy for Archer to believe his species thought nothing of genocide. "Usually, they have to go out and *find* ships to replenish their labor force!"

Archer reached the door, pulled the handle—and reacted as the door remained firmly in position. It had been locked. Out of futile frustration, he lifted his fists and pommeled the thick, unyielding metal.

The Xindi laughed—not at all kindly. "You flew right into their trap!"

Archer ignored him and instead reached for his communicator and flipped it open. "Archer to *Enterprise.*"

Static, nothing more. Yet only a moment ago, he had been speaking with T'Pol.

"*Enterprise*, respond," Archer demanded, though he knew it would do no good.

More static. Archer snapped the communicator closed.

The Xindi spoke again; this time, the derision had fled his tone. Apparently, he'd done some fast thinking. "Under normal circumstances, you might consider waiting for your colleagues to rescue you. But it sounds like they're about to become quite busy. . . ." His expression intent, he took a step toward Archer. "If you have a shuttlepod on the surface, I can get you to it . . . but you'll have to take me with you."

Archer shared a glance with Trip. The Captain had been assuming that the Xindi was what he appeared to be—a prisoner, not a plant by those on his planet who might have learned of *Enterprise* and wanted to destroy it. There was also a chance that even if the Xindi *was* nothing more than a prisoner, he was capable of treachery.

Even so, Trip's gaze reflected what Archer already knew: They had no choice but to trust him.

On the *Enterprise* bridge, T'Pol had made a few deductions of her own concerning the foreman's lack of honesty. While a slight possibility remained that the warships had some mission other than attacking *Enterprise*, it was most doubtful. A likely conclusion was that mines were fueled by slave labor, and that the foreman was most eager to add to his workforce. She was somewhat annoyed with herself that the idea had not occurred to her earlier, before the Captain and Commander Tucker had gone down. Now there was the possibility they might be held as hostages.

She turned as Ensign Sato's console beeped. Sato pressed a control, listened, then reported, "There's an audio message coming in from the mine foreman."

T'Pol gave a nod. Sato understood the tactit command perfectly, and within a few seconds, the image of the foreman appeared on the main viewscreen.

T'Pol found his appearance less than impressive. It was impossible to determine the true color of the humanoid's skin, as it was covered by a layer of grime, body oils, and trellium dust.

The foreman shot her a lecherous look, then adopted an attitude of poorly feigned politeness. "I'm afraid your Captain and his associate are going to be slightly delayed. We have three cargo vessels approaching, and we've had to begin de-ionizing our landing decks."

T'Pol suspected this to be a complete lie, but decided that it was time to gather information first, before making accusations. "How long a delay?" she asked.

"No more than an hour."

T'Pol considered this, then stated, "We've detected your 'cargo ships.' They're heavily armed." So armed, in fact, they had very little room for cargo.

"Trellium is a highly valued substance," the foreman persisted, "and I'm certain you've noticed that this is not one of the friendlier regions of space."

T'Pol remained skeptical, but did not challenge the statement. "Can I talk to Captain Archer?"

The foreman blinked several times, obviously searching for an appropriate dishonest reply, and finally said, "Not at the moment. He requested to speak to one of our miners who resides on Level Twenty-two."

"I spoke with him a few minutes ago," T'Pol countered.

The humanoid shifted his weight. "Unfortunately, the de-ionizing process prevents us from communicating with the lower levels." He paused, apparently pleased with his swiftness in coming up with yet another fabrication. "I'll have him contact you as soon as he returns."

T'Pol had a choice: to tell the foreman that she failed to believe his falsehoods, or to say nothing and instead take action to foil his plot. She opted for the second, as it was more efficient and less likely to provoke extra resistance.

"Please do," she told him, then had Ensign Sato end the transmission.

She turned toward the Ensign. "Keep trying to reach the Captain." She was obliged to do so, though she doubted the effort would be successful; she was nearly convinced now that her hypothesis was correct: The Captain and Tucker were now hostages.

At his station, Lieutenant Reed spoke up. "Something doesn't smell right."

T'Pol understood the idiom and did not waste time pretending to take it literally; she agreed with Reed's assessment. She faced him. "I want you to come up with a plan to recover the Captain and Commander Tucker.

Have it in place in one hour." T'Pol paused. She knew that Lieutenant Reed had proprietary feelings about his security responsibilities, and might be reluctant to bring in the MACOs, but this was precisely the type of situation the soldiers were trained for. "Consult Major Hayes if you feel it's necessary."

Reed nodded, showing no sign of professional jealousy, and headed for the turbolift.

T'Pol turned back to her console. With its upgraded weaponry, *Enterprise* might just be able to hold off three warships; however, since she had no idea of the situation on the planet surface, she could not be as certain about their chances of rescuing Archer and the Commander.

Deep in the bowels of the mining complex, the Xindi led Archer and Trip through a dank, narrow passageway filled with thick gray-brown sludge, tinged with the ubiquitous blue.

Archer could not remember the last time he had been exposed to so many different varieties of noxious smells. The trellium had given off a sharp, eye-watering chemical smell, the miners and foreman their own pungent aromas of long-unbathed flesh; but Archer had never before breathed in an odor so vile as that of the waist-deep sludge. As he and Trip waded behind the Xindi, their hands held high lest they touch the disgusting mess, the Captain remarked, "Sewage takes on a whole different meaning when it comes from a dozen different species."

The Xindi—who had introduced himself as something

that sounded to Archer like Kessick—was not without a sense of humor. He gave a wry little grimace and stated, "Thirty-one, to be exact."

His manner had changed abruptly from hostile and scathing to cooperative; from what Archer had seen, he could understand how years in the mines could harden anyone. Given that the Xindi had been tortured and lost a finger, the Captain could understand his initial distrust.

Once he found Kessick's people, there had to be a way to start a dialog, a way to bring about peace, to change the future.

Kessick paused; Archer followed the Xindi's gaze to a hatch resting at chest level.

"Help me with this," the Xindi said.

Archer took one end of the wheel, Kessick the other; they began to turn. Despite the desperate circumstances, Archer found it mildly amusing that, so many light-years from Earth, alien hands had designed the hatch to open and close using the old "righty-tighty-lefty-loosey" principle.

It was far from easy work; Archer gritted his teeth and strained as hard as he could; Kessick seemed equally matched in terms of strength, and struggled as well until the wheel began to loosen with a high-pitched squeal.

Gasping, Kessick nodded at Trip. "There's a lever below your knees. Pull it up."

The corners of Trip's mouth melted downward in pure disgust; nevertheless, he plunged an arm down into the viscous, malodorous waste and began groping. His eyes narrowed and his nostrils widened until Archer thought he would retch—but Trip keep resolutely feeling about until he caught hold of something, and pulled.

With a slight rumble, the hatch swung open, revealing a blessedly dry shaft, with rungs that led both upward and downward.

"This is Plasma Duct Thirteen," Kessick explained. "It hasn't been used since I've been here."

Trip seemed suspicious. "Why is there a hatch here?"

"It's a maintenance port," the Xindi said, so matter-of-factly that Archer believed him. "There's one every eight levels."

Immediately, Kessick reached overhead, where a ratchet hung in a cradle. Without hesitating, he clamped it onto a gear in the hatch and began ratcheting with all his strength.

"What're you doing?" Archer demanded.

Once again, Kessick explained honestly as he worked; after all, Archer reflected, the Xindi wanted out of here as badly as he and Trip did. "Opening the emergency baffle . . ." He pointed upward inside the shaft. ". . . up there. It's a steel plate that locks into place during maintenance cycles."

Trip and Archer stood in the sewage—the Captain doing his best to ignore the nauseating smell—while Kessick finished his work. The last two ratchets were difficult, but the Xindi put his all into it, dropped the ratchet, then turned to the humans.

"Follow me."

He crawled up into the shaft, headed for the surface. With a nod of his chin, Archer signaled for Trip to follow next; the Captain went last of all.

Anywhere, Archer thought, *to get away from that smell . . .*

Chapter 13

In the *Enterprise* armory, Lieutenant Malcolm Reed stood next to Major Hayes, staring at the large multi-colored tactical display that included several views of the mining complex: overhead angles of the towers on the planet surface and cross-sections of the underground tunnels, living quarters, and offices, all with detailed overlays giving the specifics of each area.

Reed had disliked Hayes instantly. For one thing, the man had failed to introduce himself properly, giving only his title and surname; for another, he radiated an aura of arrogance that his overly polite demeanor could not hide.

Reed was aware that he himself was not coming into the situation unprejudiced. He and Hayes represented a long-standing tradition of animosity that had its roots in centuries-old British naval tradition, and the times when humans sailed across the sea rather than the deep reaches of space. Long ago, sailors were not allowed to bear arms aboard ship; it fell to others to carry arms; others who came to believe themselves superior in training and courage to those in the Navy: the Marines.

The Marines carried weapons while at sea, and derided the lowly, unarmed sailors.

In response, the sailors made sure the Marines' time as "guests" aboard Navy vessels was as miserable as possible. Reed, an inveterate student of military history, had read stories of how the sailors repaid the Marines' elitist attitude with practical jokes: his favorite remained one about a group of Navy men who liked to arrange dozens of marbles at the bottom of the ladders connecting the different decks.

The MACOs were the distant heirs of the Marines. And no doubt Hayes was up on his military history, as well, and knew that, a century ago, only the captain of a vessel could issue a direct command to a Marine.

But these were different times, and different circumstances—and Reed was determined to make it very, very clear to Hayes that the past had no bearing on the present. Reed was in charge of security, and Hayes therefore answered to him.

He'd tried to establish the fact right off, and already Hayes was politely—but firmly—challenging the Lieutenant's authority. The two had been in the midst of a "discussion" when Sub-Commander T'Pol entered the armory.

Hayes responded with a formal, "at attention" posture,

though he eyed her with surreptitious curiosity; apparently, he had never worked with a Vulcan before. Reed, consciously more relaxed, faced her at once. "Have you heard from the Captain?" It was hard for him to read the Vulcan; he couldn't tell from her expression or posture whether she brought good news or bad.

It turned out to be the latter. "Not yet," T'Pol responded. "And the foreman isn't responding to our hails."

"The ships?"

"Less than an hour away," the Vulcan told him. She took in the sight of Hayes—no longer at rigorous attention, but still standing ramrod straight, hands folded formally behind his back—and the tactical display. "Are you ready?"

"They're armed to the teeth down there, but it's doable," Reed said, by way of reply. Although he remained cool, Hayes's condescension irked him sufficiently enough for him to bring up the matter to T'Pol. As Archer's second-in-command, she could certainly set the Major straight about proper hierarchy aboard a starship. "We only have one bone of contention. The Major here thinks my security team is too 'valuable' to bring down and put in the line of fire. He wants to take *his* men."

Hayes could not resist presenting his side of the argument. "It's a simple matter of priorities," he said, his tone carefully neutral, professional. "If those warships get here before we return from the surface, you could find yourselves dealing with a boarding party. You'd be in far better hands with a security force who knows *Enterprise* inside and out."

Reed didn't believe Hayes was sincere for an instant; in fact, he believed the Major had been primed, even before he ever set foot in the armory, to reject whatever Reed said.

Reed looked to T'Pol for support. Precedent had to be established here and now, since Hayes clearly felt he owned the Xindi mission. If it wasn't made clear that Reed was in charge, control would slip away from him, and Hayes would soon start giving *him* orders. Reed knew the type: Give a man like Hayes a foot in the door, and he'd soon claim the whole castle and kingdom as his own.

The logo of the shark he wore on his breast somehow seemed appropriate.

"I plan to have my men back on board, *with* the Captain and Trip, well before those ships arrive," Reed stated firmly, for the sake of both Reed and T'Pol.

Hayes turned a flinty, skeptical gaze on Reed, even as his tone remained polite. "With all due respect, sir, we can't be certain of that."

Reed knew no respect was involved. Hayes's air of superiority was damnably irritating; after all, as a MACO he considered himself invincible, and probably looked on *Enterprise* security as a joke.

Reed longed to show him otherwise. A wave of hostility washed over him, but he subdued it as best he could and turned toward T'Pol, waiting.

183

"The decision is yours, Lieutenant," she said—exactly the words Reed wanted to hear. And then she added what Reed did *not* want to hear. "But I agree with Major Hayes. . . . Your team may not be back in time." Unaware of the power struggle, the Vulcan had accepted Hayes's objection at face value.

Reed yielded—partially. T'Pol was forcing him into brutal self-honesty: there was *some* merit to what Hayes what saying, and Reed could not let his intense personal dislike of the Major interfere with what was best for the ship.

At the same time, he knew perfectly well Hayes was using a valid point for the ulterior purpose of establishing power aboard *Enterprise.*

Reed came up with a reasonable compromise and turned to the Major. "Select six of your men and meet me in Launch Bay One. I'll be commanding the mission."

Deep beneath the Major's cool exterior, something flared—but his manner remained controlled, his speech precise. "Very good, sir."

He strode from the room. Reed watched him go and permitted himself a small, bitter smile. As he opened a weapons locker, then began to arm a phase-pistol with a charge, he said to T'Pol, "Coming from a military family, I've seen men like Hayes all my life."

"Lieutenant?" she asked. She clearly did not understand; Reed wondered what it was like to come from a world where personal politics were unknown. He explained; this situation would no doubt come up again in the future, and it was best that the Sub-Commander be aware.

"That had nothing to do with who knows *Enterprise* inside and out . . . it had to do with who the Major thinks is more capable of carrying out this rescue."

He locked and loaded the phase-charge; it whined with power. Gripping it, he left the armory, annoyed at himself. He had let himself be rolled over—for the sake of the ship, but rolled over, nonetheless—and he did not like it. Did not like it at all . . .

Trip Tucker moved up the vertiginous, narrow passageway and tried to distract himself from the sheer physical unpleasantness of the situation. The climb had grown arduous; the metal rungs had disappeared, leaving only indentations to be used as hand and footholds. Most of them were filled with thick blue residue that Trip had to scrape out with his fingers or toes; he figured he looked as blue as a miner by now.

The trellium haze wasn't so bad in the shaft, but the eye-watering smell of sewage clung to his uniform, damp from the waist down, and of course, after reaching down in the sludge for the lever, Trip had had to remind himself several times not to scratch his nose.

The Xindi above him didn't smell so sweet, either. The miner was barefoot, dressed in the remnants of a tunic and trousers so filth-covered, Trip could not even guess at their original color. Beneath the drying layer of sewage and the trellium dust, the Xindi's legs were covered with boils.

Kessick hadn't had an easy time of it, Trip reminded himself, listening to the miner's rattling breath, audible even above the constant loud hum of machinery. It was hard to associate this distrustful, abused creature with Lizzie's death. The guy didn't seem to know about the attack—and even if he did, that didn't make him personally responsible, or mean that he had approved. He was an individual, separate from his government.

He doesn't know, Trip kept repeating to himself. It helped to calm him, to soothe the anger that had welled up in him when the Xindi had challenged them with scathing comments. Trip had almost lost it then. It had been so easy to let grief come out as anger, to pound on the nearest scapegoat. . . . Fortunately, the Captain had been there to intervene.

And then, when Kessick realized they weren't there to hurt him, but might actually be able to help him, his entire attitude had shifted. He'd removed his rags, then later introduced himself.

It was harder to hate a person with a face and a name. Trip wondered if Kessick had any brothers or sisters.

He doesn't know. . . .

But what if he did?

Beneath him, Archer called a question up to the Xindi, who led the way.

"If this leads to the surface," Archer asked, "why didn't you use it before?"

Kessick lowered his unnervingly humanlike face so it was visible between his arms and legs, and answered, "If you're lucky enough to reach the top, you'll meet some foolish corpses who can answer that question."

Trip frowned. He could manage to keep his fury under control—but Kessick's sarcasm tested him. "What's that supposed to mean?"

"The residue in the atmosphere is thirty times more toxic than it is down here. This is the first time I've had the luxury of a ship waiting for me."

As he spoke, he scraped a thick clump of blue grime from a handhold and flicked it downward; it struck Trip square on the side of his face. Disgust overwhelmed him to the point of carelessness; he let go his grip with one arm to wipe it off. . . .

Immediately, he lost his balance. His other hand slipped free, and the sudden unequal distribution of weight forced his boots from their toeholds.

He fell downward, clawing at the slime-covered walls. His desperation was born not of fear, but of a single panicked thought.

I can't fall, I can't die, I have to see this thing through for Lizzie. . . .

He caught a swift glimpse of Archer, bracing himself lengthwise across the passageway with his feet and back. Beneath him was a dark drop down into infinity. . . .

Trip flailed, grasping at Archer's chest as he slid downward, but just missed.

Abruptly, he felt the sudden, solid grip of the Captain's hand, catching his forearm. He gave a small gasp of pain; it felt as though his shoulder was being pulled straight out of the socket, but at least he was alive.

But Archer was himself being gradually dragged down the tube by his burden.

Trip gazed up, unable to help, and watched as Archer, teeth gritted with agonizing effort, pressed his legs and back hard, harder, against the walls. At last, the two came to a full stop.

Slowly, carefully, Archer began to pull him up.

"Easy . . ." the Captain breathed. Even in the dimness, Trip could see the sweat trickling down his face.

They both managed to find handholds; Trip paused, panting, trying to gather his strength.

From high above, Kessick scolded them. "It's very slippery—you have to be more careful!"

Trip looked up at him with a fresh welling of hatred: Kessick had done nothing to help them, and now merely sounded annoyed that they were slowing down his progress. Were all Xindi so self-centered, so lacking in compassion?

"Thanks a lot," Trip said, his voice thick with disgust.

Once again, he began to climb.

The foreman sat at his desk, sucking on his inhaler and, with his free hand, busily working an outdated adding machine.

His superiors paid him a percentage for each new head he brought into the mining complex—and today was a happy one for him. He was about to bring in the largest number of heads ever. With that kind of profit, he'd be able to retire earlier than planned, and maybe even live long enough to enjoy his freedom.

He was in the midst of his calculations when the door banged open and the head guard tromped in.

"They're gone!" The guard's shout was muffled by his rebreather, but it was loud nonetheless. "All three of them."

The foreman know who *they* were without asking. He stood, chair skittering backward on the metal floor. "That's impossible." At least, he willed it to be so. He would not be that close to that kind of money and permit it to slip away.

Despite his bulk and size, the head guard seemed suddenly deflated, helpless. "We searched the entire cell perimeter."

The foreman's tone grew hard, threatening. "Post guards at their landing craft. If they get back to their starship, I'll lose nearly a hundred new workers!"

If the guard valued his life, he would not let such a thing happen.

Shuttlepod Two descended into the turbulent blue murk obscuring its destination.

Reed sat beside Hayes at the forward stations. Travis Mayweather had the helm; behind them in the jumpseats sat the MACOs, facing each other in two groups of three each.

Privately, Reed was impressed by the gear the MACOs had brought, all of it reflecting the very latest advances in technology: pulse rifles, scanners, ammo.

Reed turned to address the troops, and steadied himself as the craft experienced mild turbulence from the raging clouds.

"The lower levels are hypersaturated with ionized particles," Reed said, "so you'll have to get within a hundred meters to pick up their bio-signs."

Mayweather glanced over his shoulder at them, his expression concerned. "And we've got a little less than half an hour to do it."

The troops looked tense, but ready for action; as for Hayes, he was slightly less cocky than he'd been in front of T'Pol, but Reed still detected a look of condescension in his eyes. . . .

Coated with grit and sweat, Archer climbed up the narrow duct behind the Xindi, Kessick. Beneath them, Trip Tucker followed.

The effort of stopping Trip in mid-fall had left the Captain in a state beyond exhaustion; it had required a strength he hadn't possessed, yet had forced from his body through a desperate act of will.

And if saving a solitary soul had been nearly impossible . . .

Archer refused to finish the thought, and instead replaced it with another. *Don't give up; we're nearly there.*

Once they got there—the planet surface, then the shuttlepod, then the safety of *Enterprise*, the question remained: Could the crew of a single starship and a group of MACOs stand up against an entire world?

That question now haunted Archer's waking hours and

dreams. Trip, he knew, had been almost shattered by the death of one close to him: but Archer lived each moment with not just the potential deaths of his entire crew, but of billions. It was the reason he had forced his body beyond its limits; he was responsible for bringing Trip into the Expanse, and was damned if he was going to lose him.

Over the past six weeks, the Captain had devoted himself more and more to the gathering of data concerning his mission, to rumination on possible strategy, once they found the Xindi homeworld. He'd eventually abandoned all recreation and small pleasures, all the things psychiatrists claimed were vital to the mental health of those isolated in the far reaches of space.

Mental health was no longer one of Archer's priorities. He and Trip had given up what they called their "social hour" by unspoken mutual agreement. He now spent each evening with the terminal pulled alongside his bed, reading, studying, obsessing, Porthos curled up on his feet.

The dog hadn't been allowed on the bed—at least, not regularly, and not without Archer's special invitation. Now Porthos slept there every night. The simple, warm presence of another breathing soul, one untainted by Earth's tragedy, one unaware of the staggering gravity of *Enterprise*'s mission, gave Archer comfort. In fact, before the attack, Archer had been careful to bathe Porthos daily; it seemed inappropriate for the captain's quarters to reek of dog.

But Archer had since given the practice up: The scent of unwashed beagle smelled reassuring—of Earth, of home. The Captain fell asleep each night to the glow of the terminal, and woke early each morning lying on his side, Porthos tucked against his master's chest and stomach, a warm, snoring crescent.

Even so, Archer missed human company: He'd always enjoyed discussing the events of the day with his engineer and friend—but now, the only events left to discuss were too grim, and certainly too painful for Trip. The Captain had no desire to saddle someone else with his own burden . . . so he kept to himself, maintained a professional distance from his officers.

Such barriers weren't good, he knew, but they wouldn't last forever. They would succeed at their mission—Archer clung stubbornly to that belief—and things would return to normal, no matter how horribly surreal they were now.

We're nearly there.

Archer stared up at the silhouette of the Xindi—a symbol of both doom and hope, his skin and sparse hair stained such a deep shade of blue it was impossible to guess at his natural coloration.

Meeting Kessick face to face hadn't been easy for Trip, Archer realized: Clearly, the engineer's emotions warred within him. As much as he wanted to be fair to the Xindi, wanted not to prejudge him, the rage over his sister's death spilled out at times. Admittedly, Kessick had been far from gracious to his rescuers—a fact that had left Tucker in a sour, sullen silence.

Even so, Archer was glad he'd brought Trip: The engineer had as much, if not more, resolve than anyone else to see the Xindi safely aboard *Enterprise.*

Abruptly, Kessick stopped his ascent. Archer peered past him and saw the source of the delay: a solid metal ceiling.

The Xindi was clearly surprised and disappointed. "It's another emergency baffle."

Archer scanned the tunnel walls, careful to maintain his balance. "Then there should be another maintenance port." He began to finger the walls, scraping aside the thick mineral residue. His companions followed suit.

Finally, beneath him, Trip called out. "I think I got it."

Archer peered down past his own feet. Trip was hurriedly clearing away the muddy blue deposits to uncover what looked like a release latch.

Cautiously, Tucker braced both legs and one arm in their holds, then used one hand to pull down on the latch. It held fast, rusted by disuse and corrosion. Slowly, Trip leaned back against the tunnel, and pushed his feet hard against the opposite wall, pinning himself firmly in place. With both hands freed, he grasped the latch with both fists and pulled, groaning with the effort.

Nothing. Archer was ready to crawl down and help— but Trip started moving upward until his feet were *above* the latch.

Then, in a swift, precarious move that made the Captain catch his breath, Trip stepped onto the latch, and pushed downward with his full weight.

Stop, Archer wanted to shout, *you'll fall . . .* But he knew, like Tucker, that it was time for desperate action.

Trip bent his knees again, pressing outward with both hands against either wall, forcing his weight down again, again.

At last, the latch let go a screech; Archer glanced quickly overhead.

The metal "ceiling" was beginning to open.

A minute later, the three of them were making their way along a blessedly horizontal catwalk. It terminated in front of another sealed maintenance hatch to another tunnel leading up to the surface; Archer gave his fatigued, near-trembling muscles a silent pep talk.

Hang on; not much farther to go.

Kessick didn't even seem winded, as if this were easy work after the extreme toil in the mines. The Xindi reached the maintenance hatch and groped at the ceiling in the dimness, searching for the ratchet that surely was there. After several unsuccessful tries, his expression grew anxious.

"Looking for this?" Trip asked. Archer and the Xindi turned to see the engineer just as he picked up the ratchet, which had been propped against the wall. He tossed it to Archer, who quickly connected it to the opening mechanism and began ratcheting away.

Almost there now . . .

The foreman reached out with thin, large-knuckled fingers—each crease, each cuticle, each crescent beneath his nails outlined in a darker shade of blue—and brushed away the top layer of grit from an aging monitor screen.

The display showed a schematic of the plasma ducts in the underground mines. The operation had long used plasma as a coolant; once it became superheated, it was released through the ducts until it at last cooled, only to be recycled. Since the mines were not operating at full capacity (a situation the foreman hoped the *Enterprise* crew would help correct), several of the ducts were currently sealed off.

The foreman had imagined that the Captain and his engineer, being such fit, healthy specimens, would make fine miners; now he was beginning to have his doubts.

He directed a finger at the glowing schematic. "Duct Thirteen. They've opened two emergency baffles." It was an impressive effort, to say the least.

The head guard stood beside him. "They're nearly to the surface." The alien's deeper-than-bass growl revealed a note of concern—not for the good of the operation, the foreman knew, but for his own head. If the foreman's superiors heard that an entire starship crew had been lost, there would be hell to pay. The foreman would receive the brunt of it, but the head guard was next in line for punishment. "We should destroy their landing pod."

"It's too valuable," the foreman snapped. He furrowed his worn brow. They were using the plasma ducts; why not give them plasma? Some nice, hot, heated-to-instantly-incinerating plasma . . . He pointed to the monitor again. "How long would it take to redirect the plasma flow into that conduit."

Beneath his rebreather, the guard smiled. "I'll see to it."

He strode off, leaving the foreman to watch his future fortune trying to make its way to the planet surface.

Chapter 14

Muscles aching, Archer climbed up yet another shaft, last of the trio. His positive little mantra about being close to the surface had evolved into a slightly more desperate form: *We'd better be there soon....*

Above him, Kessick led the way. He managed to continue his ascent at the same time he glanced down past Trip at the Captain. The Xindi's tone was relentlessly curious. "You've risked your lives to learn where my homeworld is . . . because you say you have important 'business' with my people. . . . Which species?"

Archer gazed back without reply, thinking of the image of the reptilian-looking biped Phlox had reconstructed from the crashed probe. Amazing, to think that two highly intelligent species had evolved independently on the same planet. Was this a situation where the reptiles and the humanoids were at war, and the reptiles had launched the Earth probe without Kessick's people being aware of it? The Captain remained silent, unsure of the answer to the miner's question.

This served only to annoy Kessick. With supreme condescension, he demanded, "Have you ever even *met* a Xindi before today?" His snideness made Archer dislike him; he seemed oblivious to the concept of gratitude toward those who would save him. Perhaps he was incapable of ascribing honest motives to anyone. Archer tried not to assume it was a racial characteristic, but instead an individual one, honed by Kessick's time in the mines. Anyone who had to deal with the foreman on a regular basis had good reason not to trust people.

"One," Archer finally answered. "And he didn't look very much like you."

Kessick's manner changed again, becoming abruptly open and unaffected; he seemed to appreciate Archer's honest manner. "Not all of them do," he explained. "There are five distinct species of Xindi . . ." His tone grew wry, and a bit self-deprecating. " . . .and five distinct opinions on which one is dominant." Archer detected a tongue-in-cheek sense of humor that gave him hope: Perhaps it would be possible after all to establish rapport with this alien. Maybe Kessick hadn't hardened beyond all hope. Maybe—and it was a big maybe—he could even be told the truth, and be convinced to help for the good of both planets, Earth and the Xindi homeworld.

Archer found the thought of five intelligent species evolving together inconceivable. He opened his mouth to ask further about the fact, but was interrupted by the distant sound of metal sliding against metal.

All three of them stopped climbing and looked down, toward the sound's source.

"What was that?" Trip demanded.

Archer began to respond—but his first word was drowned out by a second identical sound, then a third. As the last sound, coming from somewhere high *above* them, died down, Archer spoke.

"That sounded an awful lot like those emergency baffles we opened."

Trip was frowning. "Why would they be opening the rest? It'll just help us get—"

He broke off in midstatement as an ominous rumbling sound echoed through the shaft. Archer understood at once what was going on; he yelled, furious, at Kessick. Had the Xindi set them up?

"I thought you said this duct isn't used anymore!"

But Kessick's terror seemed all too real. "It isn't! They've obviously rerouted the plasma!"

The rumble had become a roar. Archer turned his face upward toward the Xindi, and shouted, "How far up to the next maintenance hatch?" Too far, and they were cooked.

Kessick blinked rapidly, his mouth working; no sound emerged.

"*How far?*" Archer's tone grew shrill, demanding.

"I don't know!" The alien was clearly panicking; he gripped the wall, too frightened to move up or down.

199

Trip, however, was all business as he called down to the Captain. "I think the safest bet is to head back down to the last one!"

"I think you're right," Archer called up. Together, the two men began to crawl swiftly downward. The rumbling sound grew ominously closer.

Kessick, however, continued to cling to the wall, petrified. "That's where the plasma's coming from! We should go *up!*"

Archer didn't stop moving down. "Suit yourself!"

He was betting that Kessick would follow. Even if the Xindi didn't, there was no point in Archer dying in order to save a possible lead. *Enterprise* was in the Expanse; she was bound to encounter other Xindis.

His first instincts were right; an instant later, Kessick frantically began to crawl after them.

Fatigue entirely forgotten, Archer climbed down as fast as he could without completely losing his grip; it was treacherous going, as the thick residue on the sides of the shaft was slippery. Within seconds, the tunnel seemed to brighten slightly; the Captain looked down and saw the distant, white-hot glow of superheated plasma.

Kessick had scrabbled so quickly down the shaft that he was now just behind Trip. The Xindi, too, caught sight of the approaching plasma, and cried out, "It's too late! We'll be killed!"

His cowardice wasn't winning him any points.

"Shut up," Trip shouted with disgust, above the

plasma's roar, "just shut up!" His tone made clear that he hadn't come this far to become another tragic victim.

Archer kept blinking, dazzled by the plasma's sunlike brilliance. Its presence gave him precisely one advantage: he could clearly see below him the partially opened maintenance hatch that led to the catwalk.

"I can see it!" he yelled up to the other two. "It's just another ten meters!"

And then he saw the roiling plasma surge forward: Just another ten meters was too far. At this rate, they'd never make it.

Like Trip, he wasn't in the mood to be another victim. "We're gonna have to pick up the pace, gentlemen!"

Archer braced his arms and legs against the walls of the duct and began to slide at a dizzying pace; he forced himself not to look down. He could hear Trip just above him, boots and hands scraping against the slick surface as he, too, let himself go into a slide.

The hatch door was there before the Captain expected it; he barely managed to grab hold of it with a lurch that jarred his entire skeleton, then he swung himself inside. He turned around at once, ready to help Trip.

Tucker arrived a heartbeat later and grabbed the door. . . .

Kessick came crashing atop him in a free fall, nearly knocking both of them down into the fast-moving torrent of plasma. Trip struggled to regain his grip on the door; as if the engineer were a rope, Kessick pushed him down and started crawling over him toward the hatch, clearly willing to send Trip sailing down to his doom if it bought the Xindi's survival.

Trip fought back, maintaining a handhold on the door out of sheer cussedness. "Wait a minute, what the hell are you—!" He used his other arm to push Kessick back, to wait his turn.

The Xindi flailed at him. "Let go of me!"

The roar was deafening now; the two men fought and cursed each other, but Archer could no longer hear their words. He leaned forward out of the hatch, feeling the heat of the encroaching plasma on his face, and saw Kessick kicking Trip in a bid to gain leverage to reach the hatch floor.

Archer was strongly tempted to leave the Xindi behind—but they had made it thus far. He leaned forward even farther, and with Herculean effort, seized each man by an arm and dragged them inside.

They had just enough time to brace themselves behind the metal door as the plasma rushed upward past the open hatch. Archer closed his eyes, but still saw the star-hot glow; the image remained a time after the plasma passed, and he opened his eyes again.

Together, he and Trip pushed the hatch closed; nearby, Kessick collapsed on the floor, gasping, exhausted from his impressive display of cowardice.

Trip whirled on him. "You stupid son of a bitch! I oughta open this hatch and throw you . . ."

He trailed off, not because his anger had died down, Archer realized, but because of the odd, wide-eyed look of surprise on Kessick's face. The Xindi was looking past them, at something he did not particularly want to see.

Archer suspected *he* didn't particularly want to see it either, but he turned nonetheless.

Behind them stood four of the towering alien guards, holding large, glowing pulse-weapons.

Kessick pushed himself to his knees.

"They forced me to come with them!" he said, his manner disconcertingly convincing. "They said they'd kill me if I didn't!" He pointed accusingly at Trip. "Just now . . . this one . . . he tried to push me into the plasma! He said they didn't need me anymore!" The Xindi paused, folding his hands together in front of his breast; his tone grew placating. "Thank you, thank you! If you hadn't been waiting here, I don't know what—"

Archer applauded mentally as one of the guards struck Kessick's head with his rifle butt; the Xindi fell backwards, dazed.

"Pick him up," the tallest of the guards ordered Archer and Trip.

The two humans complied.

The guard, clearly in command of the others, motioned for them to carry Kessick back across the catwalk. Wheezing with the effort, Archer stared grimly across the Xindi's limp form at Trip Tucker. Things weren't looking too good for them right now; the Captain silently cursed the fact that he could no longer communicate with the ship, no longer ask for backup. He could do nothing now except trust T'Pol to get *Enterprise* out of harm's way before the warships arrived, even though he knew she would be powerfully drawn to stay and wait for the Captain and Trip to return on the shuttlepod.

They stepped from the catwalk onto a landing; abruptly, the head guard came to a stop, and motioned for the others to do the same.

Out of the indigo haze, the foreman emerged, flanked by three more guards.

Archer looked on the weasel with undisguised loathing.

All unctuous pretense gone, the grimy little man stepped forward, clearly annoyed. "I would've preferred having the two of you join your fellow crew members as new additions to my workforce," he told Archer, "but you've turned out to be more trouble than you're worth." He turned and gazed up at the head guard. "Select a detail and take them to the surface." He gave Kessick, who now stood unsteadily on his feet, a disgusted look, then once more addressed the guard. "Shoot all three of them."

The words caused Archer's stomach to knot; they were not what he'd anticipated. He'd expected the weasel to order them back down to the workers' area, where Archer and Trip would have been free to plot another escape attempt.

Now time was running out. The Captain gazed up at the burly, towering aliens with their glowing rifles and tried to come up with a plan to overpower them—in vain.

Meanwhile, the head guard nodded to two of his men, who then motioned for their prisoners to head for an iron stairwell. Archer paused, reluctant.

He couldn't let it end quickly, like this. He didn't mind dying—in fact, it had always been his hope that he would die on an adventure, out in space—but right now, his mission was far too important. Death would be too much like surrendering. He *had* to think of something. Maybe if he signaled Trip, pretended to faint, allowing Trip to come over to him and distract the guards . . . It was a long shot, but he couldn't just give up without fighting.

T'Pol, I hope you've quit waiting and gotten my ship the hell out of here. . . .

At last, slowly, he turned as directed, catching a final glimpse of the remaining guards with the foreman, who stood, blue-stained fists on his hips, watching the proceedings with satisfaction.

Archer caught a glimpse, as well, of a fast-moving shadows overhead. His initial instinct was to glance up; fortunately, his second instinct, to pretend he'd seen nothing, allowed him to suppress the first in time. Once again, he prayed to a particular Vulcan.

T'Pol. Damned if she doesn't have one of the strongest human intuitions I've ever encountered. . . .

Archer kept moving forward until he heard the blast of a pulse weapon behind him.

He whirled, just in time to see one of the foreman's guards lurching backward, midsection lit up by a brilliant volley of pulses.

Between Archer and the foreman stood three MACOs in silvery-gray camouflage, each letting loose rapid streams of dazzling pulses from pulse rifles even more fearsome-looking than the guards'. The scene possessed a surrealistic beauty as the weapons' fire intermittently lit up the faintly swirling blue haze.

The weasel's guards fired back, but the MACOs' insistent barrage forced their retreat; meantime, the foreman himself dashed into the shadows.

The Captain wasted no time; neither did Trip Tucker. They instinctively worked together, taking advantage of the surprise attack to tackle the guard nearest them to the metal floor. Archer took his rifle, and barely had time to heft it before a different alien guard came charging at him, ready to shoot.

But Archer fired first, intentionally hitting the alien in the shoulder—enough to take him out of the fray, not enough to kill. Trip rushed to the fallen guard at once and snagged his weapon; together, the two of them moved through the murk toward the battle.

Archer's breath and pulse quickened; he experienced, as he often did during combat, a sense of time slowing. Although several events happened simultaneously in an instant, Archer saw each one in full detail.

In the midst of the fight, Kessick dropped to his belly and began crawling for cover.

At the same time, one of the MACOs moved confidently through the haze, golden-bright fire streaming from the barrel of his weapon. Abruptly, a stray energy pulse struck his thigh; the silvery fabric of his jumpsuit dissolved, blackened; the young man grunted, teeth clenched, as the pulse seared a hole into his flesh. The force of the blow propelled him backwards, spine curving in a "C," but his training made him keep his grip on his weapon.

Meantime, two alien guards had chosen to abandon their less-than-trustworthy leader, and were running away down the dark, mist-filled tunnel . . . only to encounter two MACOs, one of whom Archer recognized instantly as Major Hayes. The aliens raised their weapons to fire—a split second too late. The MACOs blasted them out of the way.

Yet another MACO made his way cautiously through the gloom. Out of the haze, an alien guard appeared behind him, and brought down the butt of his rifle with skull-crushing force.

Astoundingly, the MACO stayed on his feet—but dropped his weapon. Once again, the guard hefted his rifle above his head, intending to bring it down again, this time with a killing blow . . . But the MACO whirled away from him, seized a baton from his belt, and aimed it; it emitted a crackling beam that deflected the blow. In less than a second, the MACO moved in again, again unleashing a series of beams from the baton that brought the guard to the ground.

During all this, Trip had managed to shield himself behind a corroded, trellium-encrusted piece of mining equipment, and now took careful shots at the guards. As he crouched, there came a blinding explosion, a spray of shrapnel; by the time Trip opened his eyes, he found himself exposed and vulnerable, the equipment in shambles around him.

And the head guard stood a short distance away, taking aim directly at Trip's head.

But before the alien could fire, a MACO stepped up behind him, and in a skilled, graceful move, applied the butt of his rifle to the back of the alien's skull, bringing the head guard down.

Trip nodded his thanks; the MACO replied curtly with the same gesture.

All these events occurred in the time it took Archer to rush to the first downed MACO, swing the wounded man's arm over his, Archer's, shoulder, and help him to his feet.

A sudden flash lit up the dark chamber as if they all stood in full daylight; a rattling boom pained the Captain's ears, caused the metal flooring beneath his feet to shudder. Debris fell from the stairwell, followed by the sound of rapid footfall.

Along with Trip and the unengaged MACOs, Archer turned with his burden to face the stairs, and lifted the weapon in his free hand, ready to fire.

But the fresh contingent of alien guards he expected never materialized; instead, Reed and two more MACOs came dashing down the stairs.

His voice bright with triumph, Reed called down to the Captain. "It took a little doing, sir, but we've 'unlocked' the outer hatch!"

Archer lowered the rifle and deflated with a sigh, then nodded to other MACOs and Trip. Gratefully, the Captain made his way along with the wounded soldier to the stairs.

Just as he reached the landing, Kessick stepped from the shadows to join them.

Archer spoke, face, voice, and eyes like flint. "Where the hell do you think you're going?"

The Xindi had the gall to sound indignant. "You promised to take me away from here!"

"That was before your little performance back there!" Trip's eyes were narrowed, his expression taut with a disgust that verged on hatred.

Kessick held out both hands to Archer. "Please!" The exclamation hovered somewhere between a demand and a prayer. "You have to help me!"

"You had your chance," Archer said coldly. In fact, he was still desperate to get the coordinates of the Xindi's planet, but there was no need for Kessick to know that. The alien had already shown he could not be trusted; he would only share the truth if he were frightened into it.

Kessick's tone revealed only pure desperation now. "The coordinates of my homeworld . . . if you want them, you'll have to take me with you!"

"You're lying." Archer began to turn away.

"No . . ." Kessick's face contorted; he was near weeping. "I promise you . . ."

Archer hesitated. A part of him wanted to leave the Xindi behind; Kessick would only continue to lie, and if he found out the truth of *Enterprise*'s mission, there was a good chance he would attempt to contact his people and endanger the ship. Besides, his behavior had certainly not earned him freedom.

At the same time, the coordinates of the Xindi homeworld were vital to the mission. Archer made a decision: He would get the information from Kessick immediately upon return to the *Enterprise*, then unceremoniously dump the alien in the brig.

He directed a reluctant nod at the Xindi, who didn't even have the good graces to thank him.

Chapter 15

Minutes later, the group was trudging their way, heads down, into the stinging wind and corrosive toxic fog on the planet surface. Archer had already pushed his body far past its limits, but the burden of the wounded MACO was one he was glad to bear, and the realization that they had made their escape gave him renewed strength. Just behind him, Major Hayes was helping another wounded soldier across the forbidding terrain. The Captain was more grateful than ever for the presence of the MACOs on his ship; as far as he was concerned, they'd already earned their keep.

For the first time since they'd entered the Expanse, Archer felt an overwhelming surge of optimism. Whatever it took, he'd get the information from Kessick, and learn all that he could about the Xindi as a people. The mission was actually going to succeed, and it would not be all that long before *Enterprise* returned home, triumphant.

The wind roared past the Captain's ears, combining with the rumble of the mining machinery; even so, Archer could hear Reed, just ahead of him, screaming into his communicator.

"Reed to Mayweather!"

"Go ahead."

"We've got them!" Reed shouted. "Lock onto my location and set down!"

"Understood."

Reed snapped his communicator shut just as Trip made it to Shuttlepod One and opened the hatch. Archer and Hayes began to help the two wounded MACOs inside; the others squinted vainly up through the opaque clouds for Shuttlepod Two.

Abruptly, a blazing pulse hit the powdery cobalt sand by Archer's foot; he crouched slightly, shifting the wounded MACO in his grasp toward the shuttlepod hatch, then shielding him with his body. Another energy pulse struck the smooth, shiny surface of the pod, reflecting dazzlingly; soon, a barrage fell from above like deadly rain.

Archer looked above, but it was impossible to see who was firing at them—like trying to look out from the inside of a tornado. Even so, he had no doubt as to who was responsible: the greedy little weasel, still eager to get his hands on a hundred fresh workers.

The MACOs immediately took up positions around 'Pod One, and readied their rifles.

Another series of pulses zinged around them; Archer

heard a sudden shrill cry, and glanced up to see Kessick lying against the ground, limbs writhing, his body encased by crackling bolts of energy.

No, the Captain thought fiercely. It couldn't happen; the Xindi couldn't die, not now, when they were so close to getting the location of his home. . . .

Across the open hatch from Archer, Hayes settled his wounded man carefully against the shuttlepod, then lifted his weapon and tapped a control near the trigger. Archer watched in amazement as a sleek targeting scope automatically emerged from the barrel of the weapon and locked into place near the Major's eye.

Deliberately, Hayes took aim, then adjusted a control on the scope. He paused.

Impossible, Archer thought. *There's no possible way he can see through this mess . . .*

More energy pulses zinged around the Captain's feet, but he said nothing, merely kept his gaze focused on Hayes, who took his time with admirable coolness.

And then, releasing a slow, even breath, Hayes squeezed the trigger and fired a single shot . . . then lowered his rifle, a look of satisfaction on his face.

No further shots came. Archer did not need to ask what he already instinctively knew: The weasel was down, for good.

Overhead, nearby engines roared. Archer turned and saw, with gratitude, the landing lights of Shuttlepod Two glowing through the thick haze.

The crackling energy field around Kessick had disappeared; the Xindi still lay motionless, but Archer could see he still breathed. He had survived. . . .

Only then did the Captain allow himself to realize how badly he ached, how vile he smelled; he longed suddenly for the simple comforts of a bath, and a bed prewarmed by a dog.

Aboard *Enterprise*, T'Pol sat in the captain's chair, keenly aware of the approaching "cargo vessels" and the long silence that had ensued after Reed had reported the rescue was a success. Quite possibly, the team had encountered further resistance.

The others on the bridge were aware of it, too: Hoshi Sato's brow was lined with tension, though her expression was otherwise composed; at the helm, Ensign Leila Birani occasionally forgot herself and nervously twirled a dark lock of hair.

T'Pol, of course, remained emotionless—but found the current situation less than agreeable. If the so-called freighters arrived before the shuttlepods did, T'Pol would be forced to take the logical course: leave the area. Her first responsibility lay with the remaining eighty crew members aboard *Enterprise;* she was bound to protect them, and the ship, at all costs. It was the decision Captain Archer would want her to make.

After all, it would be of little help to the shuttlepods to arrive at *Enterprise*'s coordinates only to find dust, scorched debris (T'Pol had no intention of letting the ship be boarded, and its crew captured), and three warships awaiting them. In either scenario—whether *Enterprise* left or stayed—the shuttlepods would be destroyed.

It was not, however, a choice T'Pol wanted to make.

She glanced over at Ensign Sato's station as the companel beeped. Hoshi leaned forward, eager, and listened to the incoming message. She turned to T'Pol, her brow suddenly slack with relief. "Both shuttlepods have left the surface."

"Is everybody aboard?" T'Pol asked at once.

Hoshi checked her board, then glanced up again, her expression frankly puzzled. "Everybody plus one."

T'Pol tilted her head, curious. She had heard, from both Doctor Phlox and Captain Archer, about the severed finger that contained humanoidlike epithelial cells, yet possessed DNA strikingly similar to that of the possibly Xindi reptilian scales. Had the Captain managed to bring the finger's original owner? If so, that would aid their mission tremendously.

In the meantime, there were other concerns to be dealt with. "The warships?" she asked Sato.

"Still at warp four," the Ensign reported. "ETA . . ." She paused to check her console, then looked up at T'Pol again. "Approximately seven minutes."

It would be enough time, the Vulcan knew, *if* no time was wasted. "Tell the pods to dock simultaneously," she ordered Sato, then addressed herself to Ensign Birani at the helm. "Prepare to go to maximum warp."

It appeared T'Pol would not have to make the undesirable decision to abandon the shuttlepods; were she human, she might have admitted feeling something suspiciously akin to gratitude.

Inside Shuttlepod One, Archer watched as *Enterprise* loomed large on the screen; a slight shudder passed through the pod as the starship's docking arms firmly latched onto the pod.

Shuttlepod Two was visible directly alongside as it, too, was being pulled smoothly into the launch bay.

They'd made it. Archer could scarcely believe it now—though he'd doggedly forced himself to cling to hope during the experience, to increase his chances of survival. If this kind of experience was standard operating procedure for the Expanse, then they were damned lucky to have the MACOs on board.

Actually, Archer added wryly to himself, *in this case, we were just damned lucky, period.* If the MACOs had arrived only a few seconds later, he and Trip—

He deliberately stopped the train of thought. At least they were back on *Enterprise,* with a good chance of outrunning the warships the weasel had sent to capture them. That alone was reason to be cheerful.

But he was less optimistic about Kessick. The Xindi had remained unconscious through the ride back to the starship; once they'd passed through the turbulent planetary atmosphere, the MACOs had administered first aid to their wounded, while Hayes himself had examined Kessick. The Major had shaken his head. "A lot of internal damage. Doesn't look good."

"Doctor Phlox is capable of some pretty amazing things," Archer had countered. He was sitting next to Trip, who remained strapped in his seat, eyes closed, hands resting on knees. Archer worried how his friend would react if the Xindi died—but at the moment, Trip remained stoic, motionless, apparently unconcerned.

But Archer hadn't been prepared at that moment to accept that he and Trip had endured everything on that planet, endangered the ship and crew, and caused two MACOs to be wounded, all for nothing. He'd moved to Kessick's still form and leaned over him.

"Wake up. Talk to me. I need those coordinates . . ."

When no response came, he'd put his hands on the Xindi's shoulders and shaken him gently. "Kessick. The coordinates . . ."

Hayes had stopped him with a look that was firm, but not unkind. "He's severely wounded and unconscious, sir. He's going to need your doctor's help to be able to speak."

Archer had nodded and turned away, bitter; only then did he catch sight of Trip's face. The engineer's eyes had flickered open, briefly, to reveal a gaze that was haunted.

Behind them, the bay doors slid shut, and *Enterprise* leapt into warp.

Captain's Starlog, supplemental. The three alien warships followed Enterprise for nearly an hour, but couldn't keep up with us. I guess they'll have to look elsewhere for new additions to their "labor force."

As the door to his ready room chimed, Archer stopped his recording and folded his hands on his desk. "Come in." There was something very close to a lilt in his voice; he'd had that shower and a good night's sleep next to a warm dog and was feeling cheerful, despite the circumstances.

Phlox entered. The Captain knew at once from the look on the doctor's face what he was going to say; he'd warned Archer of the likelihood yesterday evening, when Kessick had arrived in sickbay. "I'm terribly sorry, Captain, but there was nothing I could do." Phlox's tone and expression were somber, slightly haggard; Archer knew the doctor's desire to save the Xindi sprang entirely from his sense of ethics and compassion, and had little to do with Kessick's usefulness. Phlox would have worked just as hard to save any other patient.

Although Archer had spent a great deal of time trying to prepare himself for this eventuality, it still stung. They had been so close to discovering the location of Kessick's world, had risked so much . . . and now they were back to square one. He rubbed a weary hand across his eyes, feeling the morning's optimism evaporate, replaced by a wave of futility.

This wasn't one piece of news he was eager to share with Trip Tucker.

Phlox saw his disappointment, and added, "I realize how important it would've been to have a Xindi to help us."

Archer lifted his head; in a tone filled with irony, he

said, "He wasn't a particularly helpful Xindi, Doctor." He tried to comfort himself with the notion that, even if Kessick *had* survived, he probably would have refused to cooperate, would have continued to be a source of aggravation.

Phlox's expression revealed he thought otherwise. "You'd be surprised," he said, in a way that made Archer glance sharply at him. The doctor reached into a pocket and produced a padd. "It was extremely difficult and painful for him to speak, but he managed to dictate this to me before he died."

Archer took the proffered padd, not daring to believe what Phlox was clearly hinting at.

"He said you'd know what it meant," Phlox continued.

The Captain stared down at the numbers on the padd, and felt a sudden welling up of disbelief mixed with hope and wonder. "I'll be damned." He gazed up at the doctor. "They're the coordinates."

He stood, suddenly energized. With the padd in hand, he exited toward the bridge, followed by a curious Denobulan.

That evening, Trip Tucker was in a better humor than he'd been in for some time. Perhaps it had to do with the fact that *Enterprise* was currently speeding toward the coordinates of the Xindi homeworld; perhaps it had to do with the fact that Trip had finally seen some action, finally worn himself out physically, finally done something that actually mattered. Things were happening.

He actually had felt sorry to hear that Kessick had died—although he didn't know why. The Xindi had been a pretty miserable creature when alive. But at least, he'd done the right thing on his deathbed.

Trip's muscles were aching, especially his quadriceps and arms; after all that climbing, he'd felt like he'd scaled a mountain. But he actually found the fatigue pleasant as he strolled along the ship's corridor accompanied by Malcolm Reed.

"I must've been in the shower for two hours," Trip complained amiably, "and I still have that crap in my hair, under my nails . . ." He squinted down at his hands, and the faint blue crescents under each fingernail.

Reed shrugged. His voice reflected exhaustion, as well, and the absence of tension that came from completing a dangerous mission successfully. "We cleared bio-scan. That's all that matters."

"The two new guys who got hurt, are they okay?" It occurred to Trip that he'd been awfully absorbed in himself lately, and not very concerned about others.

Reed nodded. "Doc's got them back in their quarters already."

Trip was happy to hear the news; he'd felt pretty guilty about so many people risking their lives to save him. "You gotta admit, their team did a pretty impressive job down there." He said it without thinking of the impact it might have on Malcolm—until he saw the change in Reed's expression.

Oops. More than a bit of professional competition

going on there. Trip backed off as fast as he could. "Nothing *your* guys couldn't have done just as well," he added swiftly.

Reed sighed; the look of jealousy faded as he clearly struggled to be self-honest. "I'm not so sure about that," he said, his tone rueful. "They *were* impressive." He paused as they came to a fork in the corridor. "I'll see you in the morning."

Trip continued on and made his way to sickbay, where the doctor was working at his station. He glanced up as Trip entered, and graced him with one of his exaggerated Denobulan smiles.

"How are you feeling, Commander?"

"Blue," Trip deadpanned.

Phlox caught the joke immediately. "I assume you're referring to the trellium dust."

Trip grimaced slightly. "You can still see it, can't you?"

Phlox's smile and tone grew gentle. "All I see is a very exhausted chief engineer. You should get yourself a good night's sleep."

Trip remembered the previous night's dream of Lizzie full force; fighting to keep the panic from his voice, he asked, "You said you'd give me something, remember?"

Phlox nodded gravely. "Very well."

He loaded a hypospray, then moved to Trip and pressed the cold metal against the engineer's neck. There came a hiss; Trip felt nothing as the medicine penetrated his skin.

Phlox lowered the hypo, then lifted a padd from the

counter. "If you wouldn't mind, Commander . . . I promised T'Pol I'd take these bio-scans to her quarters. But I
still have quite a bit of work to do here."

"No problem, Doc." Smiling faintly, Trip took the padd.
Between the hypospray and the extreme exhaustion, he was
looking forward to a full night's sleep. "Thanks."

The instant Commander Tucker left sickbay, Phlox
moved to the nearest companel and tapped a control.
"Sickbay to T'Pol." He kept his voice low, lest someone
should overhear. While he did not like indulging in subterfuge with his patients—or of forcing unwilling others
to join in that subterfuge with him—Phlox knew of no
better way to help the Commander.

T'Pol's voice, always level and even in pitch, filtered
through the grid. "Yes, Doctor?"

"Commander Tucker's on his way to your quarters,"
Phlox warned her. "He believes I just gave him a sedative,
but it was only a placebo." He paused. "He's had a rather
difficult day. I believe you have your work cut out for you."

He ended the communication at once, before she had
a chance to protest.

The door to T'Pol's quarters slid open to reveal a sight
that disconcerted Trip more than a little: the Vulcan, her
unmistakably feminine form covered by a close-fitting
pair of pajamas, on top of which lay an open satin robe.
Behind her, the room was deep in shadow, lit only by a
few wavering candles.

He'd noticed that T'Pol was female before, of course—he'd have to have been dead not to; calling her attractive would have been an understatement. But for some reason that night, she seemed particularly . . . well, vulnerable. He noticed, for the first time, that she had let her hair grow out.

He cleared his throat, and handed her the padd, all business. "Sorry to drop by so late, but Phlox said you were expecting this." He did not meet her gaze.

"Thank you." She took the padd without looking at it, then paused. "Please . . ." She took a step back into the room, and gestured awkwardly for him to enter. "Come in."

Trip couldn't have been more surprised if she'd burst into giggles. T'Pol never socialized with the crew, and despite his "movie nights" invites she had never sought out Trip. He couldn't imagine why she would invite him in except . . .

Nah. It had to be male ego talking. She *couldn't* be coming on to him.

Even so, he was embarrassed. Doing his best to hide it, he said casually, "I don't think I'd be very good company right now." He glanced down at his fingernails. "Anyway, I'd probably stain your furniture. I still have a few more showers to take before I get all this trellium off me."

She would not take the excuse. "Please," she said, in a confidential tone. "There's something I'd like to ask you."

The request startled him; T'Pol was the type to consult the computer on any questions she had about hu-

mans. At her most desperate, she might resort to asking
Doctor Phlox. But maybe . . . Trip dismissed the idea
that she was flirting with him as far too unlikely, and decided that perhaps she had a question that only a
human could answer.

Even so, he was hardly comfortable entering the
room; with its candles and meditation pillow, it looked
like an intimate little shrine.

T'Pol gestured to a chair; he took it, and she sat opposite him.

"What's up?" he asked. Vulcans, after all, liked to be
direct.

Her question took him aback. "Do you feel my rank is
still fitting?"

Trip blinked. "Beg your pardon?"

"Captain Archer asked me to continue serving as his
first officer."

"I'm aware of that," Trip said. He didn't see what the
problem was.

T'Pol hesitated. "But now that I'm no longer a member
of the High Command, I'm not certain whether the rank
of sub-commander is appropriate." She paused. "I'd like
your opinion."

Trip found the question strange. They were on one of
the most important missions in history, one that meant
life or death for billions. For T'Pol to be worrying about
her rank at a time like this seemed . . . well, petty. Even
so, he did his best to consider the question.

"I don't know," he replied at last. "You could always

ask the Captain to give you a field commission . . . Make you a Starfleet officer . . . *Commander* T'Pol . . . That's not too different than sub-commander."

T'Pol's dark eyes, rendered exotic by high, upward-slanting cheekbones, regarded him intently for a moment. She seemed to be waiting for something. After another uncomfortable moment, she said, "I'll consider that. Thank you."

He expected her to rise, to dismiss him. When she did not, he shifted his weight a bit nervously in the chair.

"Would you like a cup of tea?" she asked.

This was getting weirder by the minute. "Thanks," Trip said, "but it might keep me up. The doctor just gave me a sedative." It was a pretty broad hint that it was time for him to leave, but instead, she took it as a conversation opener.

"You're having trouble sleeping as well?"

He looked at her in honest surprise. "I never would've pegged you as an insomniac."

She gave a short nod. "I believe the Expanse has been disrupting my REM patterns."

"Probably nothing a good hypospray won't cure." There. Now they *both* had an excuse to leave her quarters.

But she had an answer for that, too. "Vulcan science teaches us to prompt our bodies to create their *own* medicines."

"So why're you still having trouble sleeping?"

"The neural nodes that need to be stimulated are difficult to reach." She rose and turned her back to him; the robe slipped from her shoulders. "Perhaps you could help me."

Trip became aware his mouth had dropped open, and immediately closed it. The thought that she was coming on to him returned full force. "I really don't know if I can—"

Before he could make his escape, she knelt in front of his chair, facing away from him. "Three centimeters on either side of the fifth vertebra," she stated expectantly as she unbuttoned her pajama top; she lowered it, exposing her back to him.

Trip felt himself flush all the way to his hairline.

"You can apply considerable pressure," T'Pol said, waiting.

Trip hesitated. Maybe this was on the level; maybe she had just needed someone to perform this Vulcan technique on her. But if that was the case, why hadn't she simply gone to Phlox? And why come up with the phony dilemma about her rank?

He decided to go along with it anyway. He ran a finger along the bare skin covering her spine, and drew in a silent breath. He had never touched a Vulcan before; he hadn't known their skin was so warm. He began to murmur, "I'm not sure which of these is . . ."

"Right there," T'Pol said.

Trip touched the spot again to confirm it. "Right here." He placed his thumbs on either side of her spine and gently pressed.

"A little closer together," T'Pol directed.

Trip shifted his thumbs in closer.

"Harder," she said.

He pressed harder. He expected her to buckle slightly against the pressure, but she held her ground; she was very strong.

"*Harder,*" she insisted.

"If I push much harder," he protested, "I'll knock you over."

She said nothing, so he pressed harder—and she didn't budge so much as a millimeter.

"Just like that," she said. "Please continue . . ."

Trip complied. After a beat, she let go a deep breath—almost a moan—and Trip felt her body relax. He felt himself blush again at the sound; this was getting way too personal.

T'Pol turned slowly to face him. "That was far more effective than a hypospray." She pulled up her pajama top and began to button it.

"Glad to be of assistance," Trip said, in his best Boy Scout, ours-is-a-platonic-relationship manner.

T'Pol stood. "It would be only fair for me to return the favor." She paused, then said flatly, "Please disrobe."

That was the final straw; Trip was on his feet in a flash. "I'm really flattered, Sub-Commander—it's okay to call you Sub-Commander, right? And don't think that under different circumstances I wouldn't jump at the chance to—"

T'Pol interrupted, an expression of disbelief on her

227

face. "Are you implying that I'm making sexual advances?"

Maybe he'd misunderstood: Right. Just misunderstood. Regardless of what the truth was, Trip just wanted out of there, and fast. "No, no, not at all," he lied. "I . . . I was just . . . you see, the doc gave me this sedative and I think it's starting to . . ."

She cut him off again. "The doctor injected you with a *placebo*. He sent you here because he wanted *me* to persuade you to try Vulcan neuropressure. As I predicted, it was a pointless exercise." The strange awkwardness had fled her tone, replaced by a flat adamance: she clearly was displeased with herself for misleading someone.

Trip first felt an enormous sense of relief: This was the Vulcan he knew, direct and matter-of-fact, anything but intentionally seductive. His relief was quickly followed by outright anger at Phlox's subterfuge. What right did the Denobulan have to embarrass him and T'Pol like this (though she would never admit to such an emotion)? "Why didn't he just ask me?!" Trip demanded heatedly.

"He *did*," T'Pol countered. "This morning. You refused."

Trip had no memory of Phlox mentioning anything about a Vulcan technique—but then, his mind had been utterly elsewhere that morning. He'd been tense, focused on the upcoming mission, obsessing about Lizzie, about the possibility of encountering a Xindi. Maybe he'd been too quick to dismiss the doc's suggestion—if he'd even registered it—but that still didn't excuse the elaborate deception.

"So this whole thing"—his bringing T'Pol the padd, her claiming insomnia and asking him to perform the technique on her—"was just a setup!"

No wonder T'Pol had behaved so oddly, so out of character. She made a lousy liar. And here he'd gone and insinuated that she was making a pass at him . . .

"The doctor knows how intransigent you can be," T'Pol remarked.

Trip bristled at the term. "Intransigent?"

The Vulcan missed the outrage in his tone and explained, "Unwilling to try something new."

"I know what it means," Trip snapped. "But it just so happens it's not true. I'm as willing to try new things as anyone else."

T'Pol took a step toward him. "Then take off your shirt."

He opened his mouth, then closed it again, forced into silence, frustrated by the realization that he'd just allowed himself to be backed into a corner.

Damned good negotiator, that T'Pol; he wondered if she'd learned that little trick at the Vulcan Embassy. They both knew he couldn't argue with her logic. And of course, the question he now had to ask himself was, why would he want to? He'd wanted help sleeping, and here was the method Doctor Phlox thought was best; why was he fighting it?

Trip let go an inaudible sigh of surrender and began to remove his shirt; even so, he shot T'Pol a scathing glance to let her know he wasn't pleased by her verbal tactics.

He set the shirt on the chair, then knelt with his back toward her, the intimacy of the situation provoking more than a little discomfort in him.

There was a soft rustling of fabric as she knelt behind him; at the sudden touch of her fingers, fever-warm upon his skin, he fought not to shudder. The room became so silent, he could hear the soft, regular sound of her breathing mixed with his own.

She pressed with a strength that was remarkable—greater than his, if not more so, and despite the oddness of the situation, Trip felt his entire body relax suddenly, deeply. The anger he had felt toward Phlox dissolved, replaced by gratitude toward T'Pol.

The Doctor had put her in a very difficult position, and Trip's accusation that she was flirting with him certainly couldn't have made things any easier for her. She had every right to throw him out of her quarters, to give up—and yet she had persisted, beyond the point of personal discomfort and humiliating accusations, in order to help him.

She really was an amazing woman . . . and apparently unaware of her striking beauty. Trip almost chuckled to himself: What kind of an idiot had he been, thinking *she* was making a pass at him? Why, any man on board this ship would thank his lucky stars just to have her look his way . . . Ever since the first day he'd seen her—

Stop, Trip censored himself silently. *Stop it right now. She's a fellow officer, damn it, and what's more, she's* Vulcan . . .

He fought not to interpret her touch upon his skin as sensual, and failed entirely.

Chapter 16

Archer stood on the *Enterprise* bridge and felt the deck shudder ever so slightly as the ship dropped from warp to impulse power; on the main viewscreen, the stars ceased their streaming and crystallized into separate, individual orbs. The screen panned until one particular distant star was in sharp focus.

The Captain was not the only one on his feet: Trip and Reed stood nearby, joining the usual complement of T'Pol, Hoshi, and Mayweather. All of them gazed intently at the flickering star.

"Tactical Alert," Archer ordered Reed. "Stand by weapons."

The Captain had spent the previous night dreaming—restless, anxious dreams of the Xindi planet, several of them, all with different outcomes.

In one, *Enterprise* had arrived at Kessick's coordinates only to find a duplicate Earth. The ship had sailed into spacedock, where Trip Tucker's sister waved, smiling, at them. Admiral Forrest was waiting there, too, and for some reason, Archer could hear him as he said, *You've been away far too long, Jon.*

And his dad, Henry Archer, was busy being interviewed by a throng of reporters; he'd paused in midsentence to tell them, *There he is—there's my son!*

On the bridge, Trip had been angry, weeping. *Don't trust them! It's all a trick. They want us to think they're human. We've got to kill them, kill them all now . . . !*

T'Pol, in her diplomat's uniform, turning toward him slowly. *I must concur with Commander Tucker's assessment.*

A second dream had followed swiftly, a brief one in which *Enterprise* had arrived at the Xindi planet, only to find a planet filled with beautiful, gleaming cities . . . and not a single soul. A ghost planet . . .

Archer had awakened, pulse pounding, the image of *Enterprise* being blown to bits in his mind.

If they truly were going to find the Xindi homeworld, he'd worried, how would he protect his people? The Xindi were clearly technologically advanced; how close dared *Enterprise* come to their planet without putting her crew in danger?

How did Archer know an entire army wasn't waiting?

There was, of course, no way to know what awaited them. He'd known going into this mission that there were no guarantees, only hope.

The ship went to Tactical Alert; Archer turned to Reed again. "Any indications that we're being scanned?"

Reed manipulated several controls on his console, then consulted the readout; his eyebrows lifted in surprise, he gazed back up at the Captain. "No, sir. No vessels, no signs of technology . . . nothing."

This was becoming uncomfortably like one of his dreams; Archer turned toward T'Pol, who was leaning over her viewer.

"How many inhabited planets?" he asked.

She did not look up, but continued to study the readout. "I'm not detecting *any* planets, inhabited or otherwise."

Archer felt a flare of pure rage. "That son of a bitch lied to us . . ."

Trip's voice revealed both disappointment and denial. "Phlox said the Xindi used his dying breath to give us these coordinates. Why would he lie?"

Out of sheer meanness, Archer thought, but he held his tongue out of a desire not to add to Trip's hurt.

"Sir," Mayweather announced suddenly, his gaze fixed on his console, "I'm picking up a debris field."

"A ship?" Archer asked.

"It's a lot bigger than that," the helmsman replied.

"Put it up," Archer told Hoshi.

She complied. On the viewscreen, the image of the solitary star shifted, then enlarged to reveal a vast ellipsoid of debris partially encircling it.

Attention still focused on her scanner, T'Pol reported, "It's nearly eighty million kilometers long . . ." She delicately fingered a few controls, then looked up at Archer, her gaze pointed. "It was a planet."

Her words charged the bridge with excitement. Archer kept his tone even and did not permit himself to look at Tucker as he said, "Move us in closer."

He hadn't known what to expect; he had certainly not expected this.

Mayweather worked the helm; *Enterprise* responded, and sailed slowly toward the mysterious rubble.

Minutes later, Archer was still intently studying the viewscreen, which now revealed drifting debris: scorched chunks of rock, shards of metal, the remnants of what appeared to have been a civilized world.

He dared not let himself believe the obvious. There was something wrong: the debris was too scattered, over too broad an area, to be what he—and everyone else aboard the bridge—hoped. Still standing, gazing up at the screen, he addressed T'Pol. "How long ago did this happen?"

The Vulcan answered quickly; apparently, she too had sensed a discrepancy, and had already done the calculations. "Judging by the field dispersion, approximately one hundred and twenty years."

Trip was bent over a console, his tone still hopeful, despite T'Pol's pronouncement. "I'm pretty sure there was a population here, Captain." He frowned slightly at his readout. "I'm picking up refined metals and traces of alloys . . ." He met Archer's gaze with a pointed look. "Some of them match the hull of the Xindi probe."

The Captain looked back at the viewscreen, his mood

abruptly grim. Whatever this was, it wasn't the Xindi homeworld; or at least, it hadn't been for more than a century. Kessick's last words had been nothing more than another lie. The Xindi had only been on the mining colony a few years, and it was highly doubtful he'd been more than one hundred twenty years old.

This world—whether some Xindi had lived here or not—had been destroyed suddenly, violently. Speculation about what had happened here was pointless; they would only know the truth when they found those responsible for launching the probe.

"They're building a weapon," Archer said somberly, "planning to annihilate Earth because they think we're going to destroy *their* world in four hundred years. . . . How's that possible if their world doesn't exist anymore . . . *hasn't* existed for decades?"

"We know the probe that attacked Earth was built somewhere in this Expanse," T'Pol remarked, "and it was built recently. It's logical to assume the new weapon is being developed at the same location."

"But if it's not here . . ." Trip trailed off, his tone one of frank disappointment.

"Prepare to go to warp four," the Captain told Mayweather.

The helmsman looked over his shoulder. "What course, sir?"

Archer let go a breath. "We have no choice but to go deeper into the Expanse."

Reed spoke up; in his voice was a note of concern.

"Long-range sensors are showing increasing numbers of spatial distortions . . ."

Archer was unmoved. "You heard me, Travis."

Enterprise turned away from the remnants of the ruined world and trembled slightly as she jumped to warp.

In the Inner Sanctum, the primate-Xindi Degra sat at the great round table with the rest of the members and listened as the reptilian, Guruk, reported the most recent findings concerning the Earth ship.

"They scanned the debris and left," Guruk said, his forked tongue lingering on each sibilant, "nearly three hours ago."

As usual, Degra let his aide, Mallora, do most of the talking. "Their heading?" Mallora asked, his tone reflecting the concern Degra also felt. These humans, as they called themselves, were disconcertingly resilient; he had been certain that they would remain captives, mining trellium for the rest of their shortened lives, and was amazed by their escape. Their persistence was most troubling.

"Toward the Orassin distortion fields."

Guruk's answer brought sounds and gestures of approval from all ten members. The Orassin fields had great teeth, the ancient saying went, that longed to chew on ships before it spit them out.

The old marsupial Narsanyala nodded his furry gray head, pleased. "Then it's unlikely they'll survive."

Shresht, with typically insectoid agitation, released a

series of trilling chirps in such rapid succession that it took Degra a moment to mentally translate. *We can't assume that! I'm sending vessels to destroy them!*

Mallora immediately tried to calm the insectoid. "If they *are* the first wave of an invasion, it would be best for us to remain hidden . . . let them keep searching."

As expected, Narsanyala nodded once more in approval.

The aquatic, Qoh—or was it Qam—pressed his face against the transparent tank and loosed a series of mournful whistles that caused everyone to face him at once, since aquatics rarely spoke. *He's correct*, Qoh articulated, in the only language he was capable of producing. Since his pacing was much slower than Shresht's, Degra had no trouble translating this time. *They won't find what they're looking for . . . Let them keep searching.*

His statement caused an outburst of defiant chatter from the insectoids.

We're growing tired of your excuses! Shresht complained. Dark, slender limbs flailing, wings fluttering, he turned to Degra in subtle acknowledgment of what none of them would openly admit—that the primate had the most influence of them all.

Finish the weapon . . . quickly! Shresht threatened. *Or* we'll *destroy the Earth ship, whether this council approves or not!*

Degra said nothing; he was used to Shresht's temperament, and any efforts on his part to reassure the insectoid would be ignored or brushed aside. The weapon would be done when it was done—and that would be soon enough.

In the meantime, Degra was counting on the fact that even human persistence could not overcome the dangers of the Orassin distortion fields.

"Is this seat taken?" Reed asked.

He stood in the *Enterprise* mess, tray in hand; at the table before him, Major Hayes and a few of his officers were having lunch.

They rose, to the sound of chairs skittering rapidly backward, and stood at full attention as if ready for review.

"Sir," Hayes said.

Only one open place remained, between Corporals Chang and Romero; Reed settled into it. At once, the others retook their seats with admirable military precision. Romero did so with a twinge of difficulty; he'd taken a blast in the thigh back on the mining planet.

Reed directed a faint smile at them all—but the MACOs remained still, poker-faced, hands in their laps. "As you were," the lieutenant said.

He expected them to continue eating—but everyone stayed motionless. With a sigh, Reed picked up his own fork, and stabbed the piece of chicken on his plate; only then did the others pick up their utensils and recommence their meals.

Reed remembered Chang and Romero, both of whom had volunteered for the rescue operation, but there was a

face at the table he didn't recognize—a decidedly feminine one. "I don't believe we've been introduced," he
said.

Hayes remedied the situation at once. "Lieutenant
Reed," he said. "Corporal McKenzie." Once again, no
first names were involved. Reed was beginning to think
that in order to become a MACO, one had to surrender
one's given name.

"Corporal," Reed said, extending his hand. McKenzie
was a small, slight woman, sharp-chinned and lean, but
she returned Reed's grip with impressive strength.

"Sir," she said.

He felt he should say something more—*pleasure,* or
charmed—but the MACOs would probably deem it inappropriate, too civilian. He broke off contact, then turned
to the dark-haired Romero, who was making swift work
of a nicely British meat-and-potatoes lunch. "Good to see
you up and about, Corporal."

Romero shrugged. "Wasn't that serious, sir."

Ah, yes, Reed thought, *"Ever Invincible." Can't admit
we're human* . . . Even so, he was grateful to the young
man for his bravery under fire.

Romero continued. "Anyway, your CMO's very good at
his job. A little strange—but pretty good."

"Doctor Phlox, yes." Reed smiled. "I must agree with
you on both accounts there."

An awkward silence passed. Finally, Major Hayes
asked, "What's our heading now, sir? I understand the
coordinates the Xindi gave us didn't exactly pan out."

Interesting, Reed thought, that Hayes managed to stay so informed about what was happening aboard *Enterprise*. Technically, there was no liaison other than the Captain with the authority to share this kind of information with the MACOs—a situation which would need to be remedied. "No," he admitted glumly. "We're heading further into the Expanse." He paused. "You might want to prepare your people, Major. We're headed into an area of spatial distortion."

Hayes lifted his eyebrows questioningly.

"It means we're in for a bit of a bumpy ride," Reed explained. He paused, then lowered his voice. If he and Hayes were to work together for an indefinite length of time, a level of detente had to be established. "Look, I just wanted to commend you"—he glanced around the table—"all of you, for your performance down on the planet surface. Well done."

Hayes regarded him silently for a moment; the major's expression relaxed only slightly as he registered and appreciated the compliment, then grew guarded again. "We were just doing our jobs, sir. Nothing out of the ordinary."

Reed stared back at him. Hayes was a rock: implacable, immutable, incapable of giving an inch. No matter what Reed said or did, the major would always challenge his authority, would always want to be in charge of every away mission. It was in his nature.

And, Reed reflected, if their positions were reversed, he, Reed, would do exactly the same thing.

"Even so," Reed said, "I still commend you." He surrendered all further attempts at conversation and began sawing on his chicken.

Perhaps all competition with Hayes could not be avoided, but Reed would do his best in the future to ease whatever tensions existed between his security team and the MACOs.

In the meantime . . . he and a couple of his men had located some old, unused bearings . . . nice and round and slippery, like marbles. He'd learned that the MACOs had set up some ropes in a makeshift gym area, to practice scaling walls. It might be interesting to surreptitiously place a few bearings under the ropes. . . .

A little healthy rivalry was, after all, traditional.

"Thank you," Trip Tucker said, standing in the doorway to T'Pol's quarters. The Commander seemed considerably more relaxed than he had the previous night, when he'd had his first session of Vulcan neuropressure.

"I'm pleased to be of help," T'Pol said, which was quite true. Because Tucker's muscles had been less tense this evening, she'd been able to do deeper work without harming him, which would allow the treatment to be even more successful.

"How many more . . . ?" Tucker asked, lingering. It seemed to T'Pol that he was reluctant to leave; perhaps he was, as humans often were, in the mood for conversation. She wondered whether it would be appropriate to ask whether he wanted a cup of tea—then, remembering how he'd reacted to the question the night before, decided against it.

"One," T'Pol replied. "From what you've told me, you seem to be responding quite well."

Perhaps she misinterpreted his expression, but she thought she caught a fleeting look of disappointment cross his features. "Oh," he said, then gave a little half-grin. "Well, thanks again."

"Sleep well," T'Pol said, and retreated inside so that the door would close.

Once inside, she removed her civilian clothing, then reached in her closet for her pajamas.

Next to them hung the diplomat's uniform.

The sight of it made T'Pol consider her current situation. The last time she had gazed upon the uniform, she had seen it as a silent rebuke, a reminder that she had given up a career, a family, perhaps even a world.

She no longer felt the same. The barriers between her species and that of Earth no longer seemed so important; these humans were now her family, her world. And her decision to send the MACOs to the mining world—a decision she had feared was rash, impatient—had saved the Captain's and Commander Tucker's lives. She was in fact critically needed aboard *Enterprise;* her choice to abandon her diplomatic career in order to follow Archer into the Expanse had already proven useful.

And, despite the initial uncomfortable misunderstanding, she was glad to be of help to Commander Tucker. While he was definitely prone to strong emotions, he was also intelligent and considerate, capable of a great deal more compassion than he openly displayed. She was glad that she had not refused Phlox's request to give him neuropressure.

T'Pol stared for a moment at the diplomat's uniform in her closet, and a strangely human simile surfaced in her thoughts.

Like shedding old clothes . . .

She carefully removed the uniform from the hanger, dropped it into the recycler, and pressed the control.

It disappeared with a soft *whoosh.*

Moments later, Archer was propped up on his bed, as usual squinting at a monitor screen on a portable arm; the split display showed Phlox's representation of a reptilian-looking Xindi, a scan of Kessick's corpse, and a schematic of what they'd already mapped of the Expanse. Porthos was beside him, chin resting on his thigh as Archer slowly stroked the beagle's smooth head.

It was hard not to feel hatred for Kessick; it was as though the Xindi taunted him from beyond the grave—only adding another layer to the mystery. Did Kessick even know his world had attacked Earth? If not, why had he been so desperate, why had he struggled so painfully, to gasp out the coordinates as he was dying? Had he been a cleverly planted spy, in touch with those who had launched the probe? Or was he merely what he seemed to be, one of the weasel's captives?

The more he thought about it, the more frustrated

Archer became; when his door chimed, he jumped slightly, causing Porthos to lift his head and shoot him a baleful look.

"Come," Archer said.

To his surprise, Trip Tucker entered, holding a small, gilded portfolio and a bottle of Scotch.

"Turn that damn thing off," Tucker said amiably, with a nod at the monitor. "You'll get eyestrain." He settled into a nearby chair without invitation and set the bottle and portfolio down on a table. "You got a couple of glasses?"

"Sure," Archer said, still taken aback. He rose, pushed the monitor arm out of his way, procured the glasses, and handed one to Trip.

Trip generously filled the one in the Captain's hand first, then put less than a finger's breadth in his own.

"I hate to spoil a good party," Archer remarked as he settled back on the bed, "but . . . you sure that's good for you? It can disrupt your sleep patterns, you know."

"Phlox been tattling on me? Whatever happened to doctor-patient privilege?"

"No," the Captain said. "*You* were the one crabbing about having trouble sleeping."

Trip's good humor remained undeterred. "My sleep patterns are just fine, thank you—compliments of T'Pol. The Scotch is strictly for social enhancement."

Archer's eyebrows levitated at once. "T'Pol? Is there something I should know?"

Trip drew out the suspense; he took a long sip of his

245

drink and let it linger a moment on his tongue before replying. "She's giving me Vulcan neuropressure. It enhances the body's own ability to normalize its sleep patterns. Much more effective than drugs. One more treatment, and I'm done. Just came from her quarters."

"You mean," Archer teased, "you've been stopping by a certain young woman's quarters every night, and you didn't tell me?" Secretly, he was pleased to see Trip here, looking and sounding so much like his old self; whatever T'Pol was doing, it was working just fine. "You know, I always suspected you'd taken a little shine to her . . ."

Was it his imagination, or did Trip blush? The engineer ducked his head to take another sip, then leaned forward to scratch Porthos's rump; the dog's hind leg clawed in response at the empty air.

"Phew." Trip's nose crinkled. "No offense, old buddy, but I think you could use a bath."

Point well taken; Archer made a mental note to wash the dog. With sudden intensity, he realized just how badly he had missed his talks with Trip; maybe it *had* been a mistake, after all, to give up the socializing, the pleasantries. Maybe he needed all those things to make this experience bearable. He took a gulp of the Scotch, winced slightly at the alcoholic fumes that rose in his nose and gullet, then said what he'd been wanting to tell Trip ever since they'd discovered the destroyed planet. "I'm sorry, Trip. We failed this time around."

"What're you apologizing to me for? Besides, we

haven't failed." Tucker set down his glass. "We simply haven't gotten where we're going yet."

"That's one way to look at it." Archer let go a tired sigh. "It's just that we seemed so close."

A long pause ensued, then Trip drew in a deep breath; his voice lowered, softened. "I was wondering . . . there never was any kind of memorial service for Lizzie. I know the timing's off, and you didn't know her . . ."

Archer didn't leave him hanging for an instant. "I'd be honored to conduct a ceremony."

Tucker looked relieved. "Nothing formal, you know. Lizzie wasn't into formalities. . . . She wouldn't want a fuss. . . ." He swallowed hard, then added, "I thought just a small group. Reed, Hoshi, Mayweather, T'Pol . . ."

The Captain nodded. "We can set something up as soon as you'd like."

Trip set a hand on the portfolio, then asked, a bit shyly, "Have I ever shown you a picture of Lizzie? Any of her work?"

"No," Archer said. "I'd love to take a look." He scooted over on the bed, making room for Trip to sit next to him.

Tucker opened the portfolio to reveal the hologram of a beautiful, smiling young woman. "This is my favorite one of her," he said. Archer looked down at the picture, and smiled himself.

Outside the window, alien stars streamed past.

Printed in the United States
By Bookmasters

Printed in the United States
By Bookmasters